JACK'S BACK

Norah McClintock

Cover by
Laura Fernandez

Scholastic Canada Limited

Scholastic Canada Ltd.
123 Newkirk Road, Richmond Hill, Ontario, Canada
L4C 3G5

Scholastic Inc.
730 Broadway, New York, NY 10003, USA

Ashton Scholastic Limited
Private Bag 1, Penrose, Auckland, New Zealand

Ashton Scholastic Pty Limited
PO Box 579, Gosford, NSW 2250, Australia

Scholastic Publications Ltd.
Villiers House, Clarendon Avenue, Leamington Spa,
Warwickshire, CV32 5PR, UK

ACKNOWLEDGEMENTS

Excerpt from *Sundial of the Seasons,* reprinted by permission of Frances Collin, Literary Agent, copyright © 1964 by Hal Borland, renewed 1992 by Donal Borland.

Excerpt from *The Poetry of Robert Frost,* edited by Edward Connery Lathem, copyright © 1930, 1939, © 1969 by Holt, Rinehart and Winston. Copyright © 1958 by Robert Frost, copyright © 1967 by Lesley Frost Ballantine. Henry Holt and Company, Inc., Publisher.

Canadian Cataloguing in Publication Data

McClintock, Norah
  Jack's back

ISBN 0-590-74350-3

I. Title.

PS8575.C62J32 1992   jC813'.54   C92-094365-9
PZ7.M224Ja 1992

6 5 4 3 2 1   Printed in Canada   2 3 4 5/9
Manufactured by Webcom Limited

ONE

*"Home is the place where, when you
     have to go there
They have to take you in."*
          Robert Frost
          "The Death of the Hired Man"

1

Jack clung to the small black suitcase as if it were a life buoy and forced himself to smile at the attractive brunette who had just pressed a delicately scented cheek against his face. He tried to think of her as his mother, but the word didn't connect, even though he had been staring into her anxious eyes every day for nearly a month.

She looked as ill-at-ease in her role as he felt in his. She stood in the open doorway, her hands picking nervously at the hem of her cream-coloured cardigan sweater as she said, "I'm sorry about your father." The scent of Chanel that came off her was mixed with a second aroma, one that was grainy and slightly sour — the way Bugs smelled when he dropped by in the evenings sometimes, after a dinner of schnitzel and imported German beer. "Something came up," she said breathlessly. A little too breathlessly. "Something at the office. You know."

Jack nodded, even though he did not know.

"He'll be home for supper, though," she added. "He promised." She offered a fragile smile. "Well, don't just stand there," she said. "Come in."

"Thank you," Jack said automatically, and could have kicked himself when he saw her wince. You don't thank your mother for inviting you into your own house, stupid, he thought. You don't ring the doorbell, either, and stand on the stoop waiting for her to ask you in. But he had done that, too. He hadn't been able to bring himself to just barge on in.

"I'm sorry I couldn't come and get you," his mother said. "I'm sorry you had to take a taxi."

He wasn't at all sorry. In fact, he had been grateful for those last few minutes on his own before plunging back into a life he knew nothing about.

Now, as he stepped across the threshold onto the black and white checkerboard tile of the wide front foyer, a chill rippled up his spine.

He had been told that his father was a stockbroker. It looked to Jack as though he was a successful one. From the front hall, he could see into a room that looked like a full-page spread from *House Beautiful*. He'd often glanced through the magazine while in the waiting room of the hospital's neurology department. The pile on the rug stood higher than the grass on the lawn outside. The walls were hung with so many paintings that the living room looked like an art gallery.

Jack turned back to his mother who was standing at the foot of a highly xpolished staircase. The staircase split into two halfway up, like a pair of glossy arms reaching to the upper wings of the house. She watched him through liquid eyes.

"Are you hungry?" she asked. "Would you like me to ask Marguerite to fix you something to eat?"

"Marguerite?" The name meant nothing to him.

"The cook," his mother said. "You remember—" She broke off abruptly. A red stain rose in her cheeks as quickly as mercury in a thermometer on a hot day. "I'm sure she wouldn't mind preparing a snack for you," she added.

"No, thanks," Jack said. He shifted his small suitcase to his other hand and looked around again, wondering what it was like to live here, wondering if he had been happy. "I . . . I guess I'm sort of tired," he said at last. What was he supposed to call her? Mom? Mother? *Mommy*? None of them seemed right. So far he had got by with not calling her anything at all. He decided to continue in that vein, at least for the time being. "I think I'd like to lie down for a while."

She took the comment as criticism. The fragile smile slipped from her lips and she looked agitated.

"I'm sorry," she said. Her eyes verged on flooding. He guessed maybe she had been hoping for a second miracle. Maybe she had thought everything would work out fine once she had him home, that she would have her son back.

Jack realized that he had been hoping for the same thing, and now that it hadn't happened, he felt empty, incomplete, disappointed. There had been no sudden illumination, no blinding revelation, no miraculous epiphany.

"I should have realized you'd be tired after all you've been through. You go right up to your room, Jack. You lie down and rest. I'll call you when it's time for supper."

If you'll just direct me to my room, he wanted to say but didn't. Besides, how hard could it be to find his own room, even in a house this size?

"Thank you," he said. It came out wrong. Too stiff. Too formal. She winced again. I should never have let Bugs talk me into this, Jack thought. This isn't even my place. Not any more. It's hers, filled with her memories, not mine. And every time I don't react the way she wants or expects me to, I hurt her. The last thing I want to do is hurt my own mother, even if she is a complete stranger.

"Try it," Bugs had urged. "Give it a couple of weeks and see how it works out."

"And if it doesn't work out?"

Bugs had only shrugged. "What do you say we cross that bridge when we come to it, Jack?"

A couple of days. Each swelled to a lifetime as Jack contemplated them now. He started up the stairs, tightening his grip on his suitcase. Everything it contained could easily have been carried in a lunch bag, but on one of her visits his mother had brought it to him. "For coming home," she'd said.

"Jack?"

He turned in almost automatic answer to the name. He had progressed that far, at least.

"Second door on the right," she said. When he frowned, she added, by way of explanation, "Your room."

2

My room.

He hesitated in front of the closed door, afraid to touch the knob. *My room, and I can't even begin to imagine what it looks like, what's inside.* Don't be stupid, he told himself. What could possibly be in there? Instruments of torture? Skeletons in shackles? Decaying human body parts? Get a grip on yourself, Jack. You're a seventeen-almost-eighteen year-old suburbanite, not a *summa cum laude* from the Psychopathic School of Persuasion. He closed his eyes, twisted the knob and shoved open the door.

When he opened his eyes, he felt both foolish and relieved. His room bore no resemblance whatsoever to a medieval dungeon. It looked like a regular room. A regular upscale room, in fact. Oak bed, oak dresser, oak rocking chair, oak desk and chair, oak computer table. One wall was dominated by an entertainment centre, complete with TV, stereo, VCR, CD player. It was the kind of room he thought he could get used to inhabiting.

He closed the door. As he eased himself down onto the firm double-bed mattress, he heard a crackling sound somewhere below him. He rolled over onto his stomach, and heard the sound again. When he lay still, he heard nothing. He slipped a hand under the covers, between the mattress and the box springs, and pulled out a handful of magazines. *Playboy* magazines. And a couple of *Penthouses*.

Jack, old buddy, you have secrets, he thought. Secrets even I don't know. Or, at least, that I don't remember.

He flipped a *Playboy* open to the centrefold and admired Miss June.

3

"Jack! Ja-ack!"

He awoke with a start. Half a dozen magazines cascaded to the floor.

"Jack?"

The voice was softer now, and seemed to come from just outside his door.

"Just a minute," he called. He scrambled for the magazines and crammed them back under the mattress. "Come in," he called. To his own ears he sounded as guilty as sin.

The door opened a crack. His mother's face, adorned by a shaky smile, peeked in.

"Daddy's home," she said. "Supper's ready."

As if cued, Jack's stomach rumbled like a mine threatening to cave in. He wondered if Marguerite was a good cook.

"I could eat a bear," he said as he swung his legs over the side of the bed. "With a couple of cubs for dessert."

His mother's eyes filled with tears.

"Oh, Jack," she said, her voice quavering with excitement. Or was it longing? She had a strange look on her face, as if she were peering at him from a great distance, or over time. As if she'd seen something or heard something familiar. Maybe she had recognized something in the tilt of his head or in the enthusiastic lilt of his voice.

Whatever it was, it gave Jack the willies. It was as if she were staring at him but was seeing someone else entirely, as if he were trapped in the body of a complete stranger. Which, he realized, he was.

Suddenly he wished he was back in his single bed near the window, up on Three East. Except he had a hunch that the food that Marguerite served would be superior to the fare ladled out by the industrial-sized kitchen on Two.

It was.

In fact, Marguerite's cooking was so good that, as he ploughed through the zesty minestrone soup, as he crunched the warm crusty garlic bread, as he dug into the mound of lasagna, Jack was nearly oblivious to the man in the grey double-breasted suit on his right who was his father, and the woman in the cream-coloured cardigan to the left who was his mother. Only when he was sated did he lean back in his chair and take stock. Then he noticed that his mother's dinner sat untouched on her plate. Her fingers were twined around the stem of her wine glass. A smile trembled on her lips. Jack's father, at the other end of the table, sliced precise triangles off the end of his lasagna, deposited them neatly into his mouth, and chewed . . . four, five, six times each mouthful.

"I see you haven't lost your appetite," he said as he eyed Jack's empty plate. His smile was brittle, his tone flat. When Jack looked at him, his father immediately looked back down at his plate.

"He always had a good appetite, John," his mother said.

John. Jack knew that was his father's name. He had been told. But until that moment it had not sunk in. His father was John, which made him John Junior. Jack. Daddy's little namesake. Jack watched with the eyes of a stranger as his father finished his lasagna and dabbed at the corners of his mouth with his linen napkin.

"Marguerite made trifle for dessert," Jack's mother announced, her eyes shining as if she were presenting him with a gift.

Trifle. "Great," Jack said. He even managed a smile. He had eaten trifle once on Three East, and then it had been a mystery to him how it had turned up on his dinner tray. He didn't remember ticking it off the menu, although it was possible, of course, that he had — by mistake. It took him only one mouthful to vow it was a mistake he would never repeat.

His mother's face crumpled. "If you'd rather have something else . . . " She started out bravely, but her voice petered out like a car with a dry gas tank.

"Elise, for heaven's sake," Jack's father said, "if the boy doesn't want trifle, he doesn't have to have it. It's only a pudding, for heaven's sake."

"But it's his favourite."

His favourite? Trifle? Jack, my boy, he thought grimly, just what kind of a guy are you?

Jack's father shot his mother a look you'd need armour to protect yourself from, if looks really could kill.

"I'd love some trifle," Jack said, to keep the peace. He wasn't even hungry any more. He was coming apart at the seams from the soup and the bread and the lasagna.

Marguerite spooned him a heaping bowlful of trifle topped with whipped cream. Jack bit into it with trepidation, expecting to taste the same sticky bland wallpaper paste that had come out of the kitchen on Two. Instead his mouth tingled with rich vanilla custard, melt-in-your-mouth cream, and light fingers of sherry-soaked pound cake. Before he knew it, he was scraping his bowl clean. His mother beamed.

"You see?" she said triumphantly to his father.

John Thorne wadded his napkin and dropped it into his own bowl. "Excuse me," he said. "I have an appointment."

"John! You're not going out? Not tonight?"

Jack's father stared evenly at her. "It's business, Elise. Someone has to pay the bills around here."

He strode out of the dining room. Jack heard his heels click on the checkerboard tile in the front hall. The front door slammed, then a car engine revved in the driveway. Jack's mother burst into tears.

4

Only Elise Thorne's sniffles pierced the heavy silence that hung over the dining room. Her face was flushed, her smile weak and sheepish.

"I . . . I'm sorry," she said.

"It's okay," he replied. The words were flimsy, totally inadequate to the task of shoring her up. But what else should he say? What *could* he say that wouldn't make the situation worse? What did she expect from him? What did she want?

She pushed her smile to the brink of bravery. "Well," she said, folding her linen napkin, setting it gently onto the table as if it were a fragile creature, "I'm sure you must be tired, Jack. I know I am. It's been a long day."

Do something, Jack, he told himself. She's your mother, for pete's sake, and she's one very unhappy lady. Do something, say something to make her feel better.

"Yeah, well," he said awkwardly, peering at her, searching for a clue. She reddened under his scrutiny and started fiddling with the buttons of her cardigan. I've embarrassed her, he realized. A blush blossomed on his own cheeks. How was he supposed to react to this? What was he supposed to do? "I guess I am tired," he said at last. He pushed his chair back and stood abruptly. Coward, he thought. Running away from your own mother. Turning your back on her, for pete's sake. "I . . . I think I'll go up to my room." Coward. Is this the kind of person you used to be? The kind who'd leave a woman crying alone in an empty house?

His mother sat with her head bowed, buttoning and unbuttoning the bottom button of her cardigan.

"Well . . . " he began.

She looked up at him, her eyes filled with hope and tears.

" . . . goodnight . . . " he said. She seemed to catch her breath, and waited. But the word caught in his throat. Mother. Suppose that wasn't even the right word? Suppose he had never in his life called her mother, but Mom or Ma or, you never knew, Mommy? Her eyes were locked on him, so transparent he could see through them to her thoughts. She's waiting. Waiting for you to say it. But he couldn't force the word — any of them — to his lips.

"Goodnight," he repeated hoarsely.

She drew in a long, shuddering breath. A plump tear overspilled her eye and dribbled down her cheek. She blotted it with a finger wrapped in linen.

"Goodnight, Jack," she said quietly.

He swung the small black suitcase onto the bed. It didn't take much effort. The bag was light and didn't have much heft to it. It didn't have much in the way of contents, either.

He flipped the latches open, swung back the lid, and lifted out the pairs of new underwear his mother had brought him — the underwear that had made him suspicious (normally suspicious, Bugs had assured him) when she gave it to him. Because if he really was her son as everyone claimed, why didn't she simply bring him his old underwear from home? Not that he would have worn it, of course. That would have been like crawling into the shorts of a complete stranger.

She had also given him a new hairbrush and toothbrush, two new pairs of jeans, a couple of shirts, a couple of sweaters. Inside the bag, too, were two paperback novels by Stephen King, pressed on him by Bugs. Jack carried them to the shelf beside his desk. No problem squeezing them in there. Apart from a clutch of textbooks, the reading material of his previous existence seemed to consist mainly of *Sports Illustrated* magazines, and the *Playboys* and *Penthouses* under his bed. A real tower of power in the I.Q. department, right, Jack?

He picked up a math text and wondered what

kind of grades he had been making. His mother had told him he was a good student, but she became evasive when he pressed her for grades. He opened the book at random and found the word SHIT scrawled across two pages in scarlet ink. He flipped through more pages, then the whole book. Almost every page was inscribed with crimson expletives. At least he showed some imagination there — no two were alike. Math was obviously not his favourite subject.

He moved over to his desk and pulled open a drawer. No surprises there. Just your basic desk stuff — a couple of note pads, a half-used package of looseleaf paper, stapler, a couple of Bic pens, chewed and broken at the ends.

A half-dozen binders cluttered the second drawer. He pulled one out and flipped through it. The dog-eared pages were covered with doodles. A sheaf of mutilated test papers cascaded to the floor. History, math, English. He picked them up one by one. His heart sank with every grade he read. D-plus, D-minus, D, F, nothing as high as a C. He shoved the papers back into the binder and shut the drawer slowly. Terrific, he thought. I'm a bonehead. A permanently burned-out light bulb. The class idiot, it looks like. Ds, for pete's sake. And Fs.

From the desk he drifted over to the closet. Okay, so he had no brains. What about taste? As he grasped the double doorknobs, he prayed that

14

his head for clothes rose at least marginally above his head for math.

He swung open the doors and stepped back a moment in astonishment. The cavernous closet looked like a men's clothing store. Jeans, cords, chinos, T-shirts, silk shirts, leather jackets — three of those, for pete's sake, black, brown, and a sporty red and black two-tone — a couple of suits, even a tux. His eye came to rest on a small photograph tucked into the corner of his mirror. He picked it up and stared at a honey-haired girl with azure eyes and lush pink lips who reminded him of the blossoms on the hibiscus his mother had brought to "brighten his room." The way things are going, he thought, she'll turn out to be my sister. He flipped the picture over and read the lacy mauve handwriting on the back. *Eternally yours, Leah.*

Unless they had made radical revisions to the original blueprints for sisters, Leah wasn't one. Or, at least, she wasn't his. Thank goodness, he thought. He turned the picture over and studied the delicate face. Hello there, Leah, he thought. Wardrobe was apparently not the only area in which he had displayed good taste in his previous life. Leah whoever-she-was was top of the line, premium quality, a first-class ticket.

He carried the picture back over to his bed and sat down. This wasn't turning out at all the way he had expected — if he had really expected anything. Now that he thought about it, he wasn't at all sure he had. The last six weeks seemed, in retrospect, to have lasted no longer than a blink of an eye. He'd woken up in a hospital, and now here he was, sitting in some guy's room, staring at a picture of some guy's girl, and it just didn't make sense.

He knew he was supposed to be that guy, but he just couldn't make himself believe it, because the guy was a total stranger to him. Nothing more than a name. A jumble of vowels and consonants. And yet, like an actor thrust onto the stage in the middle of a play he had never even read, he was expected to carry out the role without knowing how the story had begun and what part he had been contracted to play — hero, villain, spear-carrier.

He stared down again at the picture. He was no scholar, he knew that now. But he must have had something going for him, because he'd managed to snag a pretty girl. He wondered idly whether she was a cheerleader.

6

Jack was sitting up in bed, propped against a couple of pillows, poring over the pages of a yearbook from Kennedy High, when he heard soft footsteps out in the hallway. He glanced at the clock-radio on his bedside table and was surprised to find that it was after eleven o'clock. It hadn't even been eight when he had found the yearbook in the back of the closet. It was from the previous year, the last year he had been in school. He had hunted around for more, from the years before, but came up empty. He'd scanned through it first, looking at the pictures and the names, searching for Leah, looking to see who she was, Leah Who, and thinking, probably dreaming, that knowing something about her might help him know something about himself.

He'd found her quickly, and once he had, it seemed as though he couldn't turn the page without encountering her again. And again. And again.

Her name was Leah Bennett and she *was* a cheerleader. She was also class secretary, and vice-president of the Girls' Athletic Association. She was in choir and tennis club, and turned up in two of the three school plays, although not in leading roles. She also worked on the school newspaper — she was listed as the Girls' Athletic Correspondent — and was pictured soaping windshields at the annual Kids for Charity car wash and selling fudge at the Red Cross pre-Christmas bake sale. He even found an essay by her in the literary section of the yearbook, a rather banal argument in favour of rules in any society, including that microcosm of it called school. Besides being pretty, Leah Bennett was a very busy girl. Jack wondered when she had managed to find any time for him, especially since he didn't seem to have been involved in any of the same activities.

He went back through the book a second time, looking for pictures of himself, and found only his class picture. He was in the back row, cross-eyed, a ridiculous smirk on his face. He glanced again at the photo of Leah Bennett, and wondered how someone like him had managed to snag someone like her.

Someone tapped on his bedroom door. Jack stiffened. It must be his mother. Quickly he reached over to his bedside table and snapped off the light. He jerked the covers out from under him, and pulled them up around his neck.

Outside in the hallway, she knocked again.

"Jack?"

Her voice was a husky whisper.

"Jack, are you still awake?"

Coward, Jack thought to himself. But he said nothing.

He heard the tiny click of the doorknob, and a wedge of light from the hallway fell across his face. His eyelids quivered. He fought the urge to clamp them shut, willing them to remain casually closed as they would be in sleep. He concentrated, too, on his breathing, slowing it down, moulding it into the long drawn-out breathing of a man in slumber, and he prayed that she wouldn't come into the room.

The light seemed to lie on his face forever. He heard soft rustling, and had to struggle to keep himself from opening his eyes to see what was happening. A gentle scent wafted towards him. A sweet scent that stirred something vague and warm inside him. He knew she was close now. He heard the small intake of her breathing, and the rustle of a garment. Her breath fell like dew on his cheeks. Then he felt her lips, soft on his skin.

"Goodnight, Jack," she whispered.

Her scent lingered in his room long after she had withdrawn.

7

For a long time, he stared at the ceiling. It was better than closing his eyes. Almost anything was better than closing his eyes. Because if he closed them, he would eventually tumble into the abyss of sleep.

And that was when it always assaulted him — a monster lying in ambush, waiting until he was at his most vulnerable, then leaping out, claws tearing at him, ripping at his mind, drawing the blood of confusion and terror until at last he woke, bathed in sweat, the night nurse at his side, her hand cool on his forehead, her voice soothing, telling him over and over, "There, Jack, it's all right. You've only had a nightmare."

Only a nightmare.

It was like saying a panther was only a pussy cat.

Here, in this strange house that everyone insisted was his home, there was no night nurse to calm him when he screamed in terror. There was no amiable orderly to pull the curtains around his bed and play a few hands of poker with him until he slipped once more beneath the glassy surface of the night. Here there was just a mother who had cried enough for one day, and who surely didn't need to cry again.

So Jack listened until the rustling of her nightclothes and the faint slap of her slippers faded in the hallway, then watched as ten long minutes reshaped themselves one by one on the display of his clock-radio. Then, when he was sure that she must be in her bed, he turned on the light and read until his eyes burned with fatigue. When, reluctantly, he switched the light off again, he still dared not sleep. So he stared up at the ceiling and wondered if the pieces of his life would ever fall into place again. Wondered if the fog would ever clear. Wondered . . .

His eyelids fluttered shut.

He sank into sleep, deeper and deeper, aware of what was happening, but helpless to do anything to stop it. *I know I'm asleep. I know this isn't real.* But knowing didn't make the fog stop swirling. Knowing didn't shake the deathly chill that crept up his spine, or keep him from cringing when the first faceless figure came at him from out of the mist.

They were all faceless, first one, then two, then, slowly congregating, a dozen, a hundred faceless figures shrouded in robes, peaked hoods pulled over their heads, casting their features into blackness. They emerged from the heavy fog as though surfacing from the depths of some bewitched lagoon, and they milled around him, closer and closer, their icy fingers plucking at him. Each touch sent a shudder up his back. His bowels turned to water. He felt as if he were about to lose all control.

Sometimes, when he woke up in the hospital, he found that was precisely what he had done. He had let himself go, and the orderly would have to come and clean up his bed while he stumbled into the bathroom and washed himself off, his cheeks burning with shame.

Finally, he was completely encircled by shadowy, faceless figures. Suddenly, as if in response to some inaudible command, they all raised a hand to him, pointing long, accusing fingers at him. And a wail came up, filled with such fury, the raging of a thousand wolves, that Jack fell whimpering to his knees in their midst. Always they would start to close in on him. Always he would look up, and one face would be revealed. One gashed and bloody face. And Jack would discover a knife in his hand, sticky and wet with blood. He raised the knife. The howling filled his ears and made his head ring.

Jack sat bolt upright in bed, his heart pounding like a bass drum. He gasped for breath as he strained to listen for the sound of approaching feet. If I screamed, he thought, she'll come running. No one came, thank God.

His sweat-soaked pyjamas were stuck to him. He flicked on the bedside light, and struggled out of bed. He peeled off his clothes. After he had mopped himself dry, he climbed into a fresh pair of pyjamas. When he crawled back into bed again, he left the light on and reached for the high school yearbook. He thumbed slowly through the pages, looking for the face from his dream. It has to be here, he thought. If I'm dreaming a face, it must be a face I remember. It just has to be here.

But it wasn't.

He drifted off to sleep again as the sun was cresting over the tops of the trees outside his window, and didn't awaken until his mother knocked on his door and called in, "Someone's here to see you, Jack."

A tall dark-haired man in a sports jacket was sitting in the living room. He got to his feet when Jack's mother ushered Jack into the room. His sharp black eyes peered deeply into Jack's.

"Jack, this is Lieutenant Mahoney," Jack's

mother said. "Lieutenant Mahoney happened to be driving by the night you had your accident. He helped that truck driver pull you from the car. You wouldn't be here today, Jack, if it wasn't for Lieutenant Mahoney."

"And that truck driver," Mahoney said. His voice was deep and rich. Seeing his modest smile softened Elise Thorne's face. "I heard you were home, Jack. I just wanted to drop by and see how you're doing."

"I'm doing fine," Jack said. Or, as he had heard Bugs say a hundred times, about as well as could be expected.

"That's good," Mahoney said. His grey eyes bored into Jack's. "Your mother tells me you still don't remember much, but that apart from that you're fit and healthy. Is that right, Jack?"

Jack nodded.

"Well, that's the important thing, isn't it?" Mahoney said. "My father always used to say, if you have your health, you have everything. As long as a man's in good health, he has the potential to accomplish anything. Without good health, well . . . " He smiled encouragingly. "Fortunately you don't have to think about that, do you, Jack?"

"No, sir," Jack said.

"Well," Mahoney said again. He smiled at Jack's mother. "I won't keep you any longer. I just wanted to see how you were doing. Good luck,

Jack." He thrust out a hand, which Jack accepted.

"Such a nice man," Jack's mother said after he had left. "I hate to think what might have happened to you if he hadn't come along when he did. Lieutenant Mahoney was the one who pulled you from the car just seconds before it exploded."

TWO

School days, I believe, are the unhappiest in the whole span of human existence.

> H.L. Mencken
> "Travail"
> *The Baltimore Evening Sun,*
> Oct. 8, 1928

Let a man once see himself as others see him, and all enthusiasm vanishes from his heart.

> Elbert Hubbard
> *The Note Book*

1

Jack started to worry at breakfast on Monday. He had known this day was coming. In fact, he had insisted on it, and his mother had made all the arrangements. But now that Monday morning had finally arrived, he couldn't help noticing that she came up with excuse after excuse to keep him at home.

That made Jack nervous. Because if she

found the idea of his going to school distressing, then he'd be a complete fool not to worry about it himself. Look how hard it had been to come home. School was bound to be worse. Far worse.

"Maybe it's too soon, Jack," his mother said. "Maybe you should take a little more time to recuperate. The doctor said you need plenty of rest."

She spoke earnestly, as if she truly believed that a few more days in bed was going to cure what it was that ailed him.

Jack's father glanced up only briefly from the pages of his *Wall Street Journal*, and then he looked directly at his wife, not at Jack. Jack had noticed that his father hardly ever looked at him. It was almost as if he were avoiding Jack.

"Besides," she continued, "the semester is almost over. You'll never be able to make up your year. Maybe it would be better if you stayed home and rested. We could get a tutor for you over the summer, couldn't we, John?"

John Thorne snapped the pages of his paper. "For heaven's sake, leave the boy alone, Elise," he said. "If he wants to go to school, let him go. Lord knows it would be a pleasant change from what used to go on around here on weekday mornings."

Jack's mother recoiled from the remark as if it had slapped her. "John, I really don't think —"

But John Thorne had already folded his

paper, drained his coffee cup, and was heading for the door.

"Will you be home for supper?" she called after him.

His only answer was to slam the front door. As his mother's eyes filled with tears, Jack uttered a silent prayer. Please don't let her cry again. I don't think I could stand it.

"If you want," Jack said, "I can stay home. I don't mind." In fact, the more he thought about it, the less he minded. How could he possibly have thought school was a good idea in the first place? He'd been living in the same house as his mother and father for three days now, and he still hadn't been able to see them as anything more than complete strangers. And what was school? Just several hundred more complete strangers, most of whom knew things about him that he could not remember. "Maybe you're right. Maybe I should rest some more."

His mother shook her head and smiled bravely at him. "I think you were right before, Jack. I think you should go. I think it's important."

No, no, he suddenly wanted to scream. I don't want to go. I've changed my mind.

"I'll drive you," she said, then looked down and seemed dismayed to find that she was still wearing her robe. "I'll just run upstairs and change. I won't be a minute . . . "

"It-it's okay," Jack said. "I'll walk." If he had

to go (and, he realized, he would have to go sooner or later, it was one of those things he and Bugs had talked about: "There'll be plenty of forks in the road, Jack, and at every one you'll have to make a decision, are you going to go forward into life, or are you going to shy away?") he intended to do it alone. He didn't want to be some mindless basket case who had to be chauffeured to school in mama's station wagon.

"Of course, you'll have to point me in the right direction."

His mother looked dubious. "It might not be easy, Jack. What if you get there and something happens?"

Jack forced a smile that he didn't feel. "What could possibly happen?" He was going off to school, for pete's sake, not off to war. How hard could it be?

2

It turned out not to be a question of degree of difficulty, but of degree of weirdness. Kennedy High looked just like its picture in the yearbook — a long, lean stretch of concrete and glass standing on a luxurious, well-groomed lawn. People clustered around it on the walkways, on the lawn, in the parking lot. And the closer he got, the more Jack felt as though he were walking upside-down in a right-side-up world.

His mouth went dry. His heart pounded in his chest. Blood rose to his cheeks. I'm scared, he realized, just like a little kid on his first day in kindergarten. I'm scared to death. I want my mommy.

He came to a stop on a corner two blocks from the school and told himself firmly to stop acting like a baby. It's just a school, for pete's sake. They're just people. Busy people, from the looks of it, knotted together in little gangs, talking, laughing, flirting — the last thing they were going to be interested in was some stringbean pale face. They probably wouldn't even notice him, right?

Wrong.

They noticed.

When he was a block from the school, a guy walking in front of him turned around. His eyes lit indifferently on Jack, and dismissed him. Then, like something right out of the Saturday morning cartoons, the guy's head froze in mid-turn and swivelled slowly back. His eyes bugged out of his head. His chin sagged and his face went pale, as if he were looking at a ghost. Jack smiled awkwardly and shrugged as if to suggest, hey, sorry, I didn't mean to spook you. The guy turned, scrambled to catch up to another guy ahead of him, and thumped him on the shoulder. Jack watched with embarrassment as the second guy also turned, popped his eyes, and almost drooled as his mouth hung open.

So much for Mr. Invisible, Jack thought grimly. A vague sense of unease washed over him. What kind of person was he, anyway, that his mere appearance aroused such shock? Don't turn chicken, he told himself angrily. You've been gone a long time, that's all. They probably thought you were dead — if they thought about you at all. Besides, what can you do about it?

Bugs always asked that question. "Sure, that's the way it is, Jack. But what can you do about it?" The answer was always the same. "You can either march right in there and deal with it. Or you can stay right where you are. Never deal with it. Hide out for the rest of your life if that's what you want, Jack. It's all up to you. Be the man with no past, if you want. Be a real Mr. Nobody." What he really meant was, be a coward, if that's what you want.

Jack drew in a deep breath, pulled back his shoulders, and started the long walk to the front door of Kennedy High. A few more people stared. Elbows nudged nearby ribcages. Heads turned. The movement progressed down the sidewalk. Like dominos toppling, attention fell from topics under discussion, and eyes shifted to Jack.

"He's back," someone whispered. "Jack's back." It was hard to tell from the speaker's inflection whether this was considered good news or bad.

More kids turned.

More kids stared.

More kids whispered.

Obviously not good news, Jack concluded. Because despite all the attention, no one rushed over to him, no one said, "Good to see you, welcome back, nice to have you on board again."

They just stared.

Suddenly coming to school seemed like a bad idea. Sort of like walking into an exam room without having done your homework. He should have done his homework. He should have found out a little more about who the hell he was before coming back here. A lion tamer didn't walk into the lion cage unprepared, did he? A soldier didn't march into battle without his weapons oiled and checked and loaded. So why the hell was he walking into some stranger's life without any preparation?

By the time he reached the foot of the walk, kids from the parking lot clear up to the front door of the school had nudged and prodded each other. Each in turn had focused in on Jack, until, like a wave, the nudge crested at the top of the steps and a dark-haired boy in a battered jean jacket turned and stared at him. Like everyone else, he blinked. Unlike everyone else, he didn't look at all surprised. If anything, he looked pleased. A smile spread across his face. He bounded down the steps and jogged over to Jack.

His grin widened as he inspected him.

"Good to see you, Jackie," he said.

Jack peered into the smoky grey eyes and saw nothing that sparked remembrance. But he recognized the thick black curls and the square jaw from the yearbook.

"Mitch Cameron, right?"

The boy looked so startled that Jack thought he had guessed incorrectly. Next time, ask, Jack told himself angrily. Don't try to be such a hotshot. In case you've forgotten, you aren't exactly blessed with the world's best memory.

"Yeah," the dark-haired boy said at last. He stared deep into Jack's eyes. "You remember me?"

"I wish," Jack said. "I saw your picture in the yearbook."

A grin washed away Mitch's surprise. "That's why I like you, Jack," he said. "You're always such a Boy Scout. Mr. Be-Prepared."

Mr. Be-Prepared? Jack thought. Me? He tried to fathom the depths of Mitch's eyes, but wasn't able to probe that deeply. Mr. Be-Prepared could be a pretty clever guy, ready for everything. Or Mr. Be-Prepared could be a real nerd — too cautious, too conservative, too fussy.

"Uh, Mitch . . . " This is going to sound stupid, thought Jack, but I don't have much choice. If he didn't ask, he might never find out. Besides, Bugs had told him over and over that there was no such thing as a stupid question, only a person stupid enough to be afraid to ask. " . . . were you and I friends?"

Mitch grinned and slapped Jack heartily on the back. "The best," he said. "You and me, Jack, we're the best of friends."

It didn't escape Jack that Mitch had used the present tense.

3

Mitch Cameron left him at the door to the administration office. "I'd love to come in with you, Jack," he said cheerfully, "but I got some business to attend to." He winked slyly. "You understand." Before Jack could say anything, Mitch was loping down the hallway, calling back over his shoulder, "Don't let Dunc give you any crap, you hear, Jack?"

Who, Jack wondered, was Dunc? And why would he want to give me any crap? As he looked through the glass into the administration office, he dug into his jacket pocket and withdrew the envelope his mother had given him. "Just give it to the principal," she had told him. "And don't worry. Everything has been arranged."

He shouldered open the door to the office and worked his way through the teachers and students milling around inside. Well, he didn't actually have to shoulder his way through. They fell away from him, the Red Sea parting in front of the Israelites. Or healthy people falling back from a leper. A little voice in Jack's head whispered, "Get out of here. Go home." The thought was tempting, but Jack shook it off. If he was ever going to find out anything, he couldn't run away.

He kept his eyes fixed straight ahead, like a blinkered mule, as he pushed his way to the counter.

"I'd like to see the principal," he said to a copper-haired assistant behind it. "I have some . . . uh . . . papers." He felt like a fool as he stumbled over his words.

The copper-haired assistant leaned across the counter, took the envelope from his hands, and opened it. She scanned the forms it contained, then smiled up at him.

"Welcome back to Kennedy High, Jack," she said. "Mr. Morris is expecting you. Come on."

She waved him through to the other side of the counter and led him to a row of glassed-in offices. She stopped in front of the corner office, and rapped on the door. The gilt lettering on it read: Duncan Morris, M. Ed. Principal.

Duncan Morris. Dunc.

Jack peered past the assistant's shoulder to a silver-haired man sitting at a well-organized desk inside. Old Dunc, Jack thought at first. But when he followed the assistant inside and got a close look at Mr. Morris, he realized that his first impression had been wrong. Duncan Morris wasn't as old as his hair colour suggested. When he stood up behind his desk, Jack saw that he was tall and fit and powerfully built. As he eyed Jack sternly, Jack wondered if he had come to teaching by way of the armed forces.

"Thank you, Marion." Mr. Morris took the envelope and the forms from the assistant, and flipped through them as she withdrew from the office, closing the door quietly after her.

Mr. Morris threw the forms down on the desk top and sat down.

"Well, Thorne," he said, leaning back in his chair, "I can't say that I expected to see you back here again."

Jack stood, since he had not been asked to sit, and was glad that he was carrying a loose-leaf binder — it gave him something to do with his hands. He waited for Mr. Morris to continue.

Mr. Morris seemed to be waiting for him.

"Well," Jack said at last, "here I am."

"Here you are," Mr. Morris repeated flatly. He shot forward in his chair so suddenly that Jack thought he was going to leap right over the desk at him. "Listen here, Thorne," he said, one long, thick index finger pounding rhythmically into the desk pad, accenting every other word, "I know you don't remember much. And I'm sure that's pretty rough . . . "

Rough? That was an understatement. Sliding buck-naked down a hill of industrial-grade sanding paper would be smooth by comparison. Jack wondered how Dunc would feel if he found himself looking into the eyes of a stranger every time he looked into the mirror. He wondered if Dunc would be able to keep his balance.

" . . . but maybe you can take the bunch of lemons that accident handed you, and turn them into lemonade. Do you understand me, Thorne? The past is the past. It's over and done with. Even if you could remember it, you wouldn't be able to change it. It's the future you should be thinking about, Thorne. A future that doesn't have to include incomplete or not-done homework assignments. A future that doesn't have to include truancies and ditching classes. A future that doesn't have to be spent shuffling back and forth between this office and the detention hall. Do you understand what I'm telling you, Thorne?"

Jack nodded, despite the tightening knot in his stomach. So far the only thing he had discovered about his former life was an antipathy for school and everything associated with it.

"Good," said Mr. Morris. He leaned back in his chair again. "It's never to late to make a fresh start, Thorne. I found that out in the Army. I've seen plenty of cases like yours . . . "

Jack blinked stupidly at him. What was he

talking about? Had he commanded platoons of amnesiacs?

" . . . guys who cruise through the world, never taking things seriously. Then one day they find out it's no joke, that if you want to get anywhere in life, you have to get serious. You can do it, Thorne. Make a fresh start. Look to the future. Do you understand what I'm telling you, Thorne?"

"Yes, sir."

Mr. Morris's smile widened. "That's the spirit, son!" he said. "Marion . . . Ms Michaelchuk will give you your timetable."

It took Jack a moment to realize that he was being dismissed. "Th-thank you, sir," he said. He started for the door.

"Oh, and Thorne?"

He turned back to Mr. Morris.

"Yes, sir?"

"Good luck, Thorne. We'll all be rooting for you."

"Yes, sir. Thank you, sir."

4

By the time Jack left the administration office armed with a timetable, a class list, and a copy of form 12A, *Students Commencing Studies After the Official Start Date*, for each of his teachers, he had missed homeroom.

"You'd better hurry," Ms Michaelchuk said. "Your first class is in Room 31. That's on the third floor, south wing."

"What wing am I in now?"

"North."

Jack tucked his 12As into his binder and headed for the stairs.

"Good luck," Ms Michaelchuk called after him. He wondered if she thought he would need it.

Math was his first class. He remembered the dismal string of Ds he had seen on his test papers and wondered if Mr. Knox, his assigned math teacher, had been his teacher before.

The last bell had rung and the hallways were deserted by the time Jack found Room 31. He hurried inside.

Mr. Knox turned out to be a balding middle-aged man in a white shirt and navy tie who was busy chalking equations of some kind on the blackboard. He glanced briefly at Jack.

"Mr. Thorne," he said, without pausing in his chalking, "I heard you were back." He spoke loudly in a voice that seemed congenial. His face was bland and impossible to read. He finished his equation and wiped the chalk from his hands. "Are you sure you want to subject yourself again to the rigours of mathematics, Mr. Thorne? As I recall, calculus was never your best subject. Final exams are only two months away. You would require nothing short of a miracle to pass."

This elicited a smatter of laughter in the classroom. Jack glanced at an acne-faced brunette who reddened and clapped a hand over her mouth. A carrot-top in the back row looked down at his desk.

"I don't expect to pass, sir," Jack said. "I expect to repeat the year."

Mr. Knox arched his eyebrows. "Sir?"

There was more laughter, and this time it was Jack who reddened. He slipped into the nearest empty seat, opened his virgin notebook, and tried to make sense of the scrawling on the blackboard.

5

Jack approached his next class with trepidation. If he was doing so abysmally in math, it was a cinch he wasn't leading the class in chemistry.

He found the chem lab easily. A muscular man in sneakers, grey flannels, and a T-shirt stood in the doorway, a whistle on a rope around his neck, and a beaker in one hand. With his free hand he was waving kids into the room.

"Come on, come on, people," he said. "We don't have all day."

But when Jack tried to hurry inside, he found his way blocked by a muscular arm.

"Where do you think you're going, Thorne?"

Jack stared at the man — Mr. Bradley, according to his timetable — and was disturbed by the hungry enthusiasm in Mr. Bradley's eyes.

"To class, sir," Jack said. He fumbled in his binder for Mr. Bradley's copy of his 12A. But Mr. Bradley was oblivious to it. He was busy inspecting Jack from head to toe.

"You've dropped a lot of weight, Thorne," Mr. Bradley said. "But I guess that's understandable. You report to me in my office later, and I'll get you back in training."

"Training, sir?"

"If you work hard, Jack, you could go out for track again in the fall. And what's this 'sir' stuff? It's Coach. It's always been Coach, right, Thorne?"

Jack wished he could remember. He felt like a man picking his way unguided through a mine field.

Mr. Bradley clapped him on the shoulder. "Don't worry, Thorne. We'll have you back in shape before you know it. Who knows, maybe after all that rest you got, you'll come back better than ever. How about that, Thorne?"

The bell rang in the deserted hallway.

"Come on, grab a seat," Mr. Bradley said. "And don't worry about the lab assignments — "

"I'd like to try," Jack said.

Mr. Bradley's brows crept up his forehead.

"Are you sure, Thorne? You've missed most

of your year already. And this wasn't exactly one of your best subjects."

It was an observation he was hearing with discouraging regularity. But he nodded.

"Okay," Mr. Bradley said. "Have it your way. You always were pig-headed — " He broke off abruptly and looked with discomfort at Jack. "I didn't mean that the way it sounded, Thorne."

Jack wasn't sure how it sounded. "It's okay," he said.

"Yeah," Mr. Bradley said. "Well, I guess we'd better get you a lab partner." He glanced around the room. "Hey, Taradash!" A black-haired girl at a rear lab bench looked up from an open textbook. She pressed a finger against her chest and mouthed the word *me?*

"Yeah, you. Congratulations, Taradash. We finally found you a lab partner."

Ms Taradash looked unimpressed as she regarded Jack.

"Just do what she tells you, Jack," Mr. Bradley said. "She knows her stuff. Maybe you'll learn something." He patted Jack encouragingly on the shoulder.

Jack made his way to the lab bench in the rear of the room.

"I'm Jack," he said.

"Cleo," she replied indifferently.

"Okay, people!" Mr. Bradley clapped his hands to get everyone's attention. "Come on, we've got a long way to go and a short time to get there."

As Mr. Bradley began his lecture, Cleo eyed Jack.

"Where'd you spend the last couple of months?" she asked. "In a closet?"

Jack looked down at himself in confusion. What did she mean? What was she talking about?

"You look like Boo Radley," she said.

Boo Radley? "Who's that?"

Her eyes widened. "You're kidding, right?"

"I don't think so."

"You never read *To Kill a Mockingbird*? It won the Pulitzer Prize!"

Jack had never heard of the book, but that didn't mean he hadn't read it.

Cleo rolled her eyes. "Great," she muttered. "I've been pulling straight As all year. And now I get saddled with a semi-literate. What kind of grades did you get at your last school, anyway?"

"Ms Taradash?" Mr. Bradley called from the front of the room. "Ms Taradash, would it be too much to ask that you pay attention?"

Cleo's cheeks turned crimson. She shot one last glance at Jack. Then she gave Mr. Bradley her undivided attention.

The bell rang. Jack consulted his timetable and breathed a sigh of relief. His next scheduled period was lunch.

He stashed his binder in his locker and retrieved the lunch bag his mother had given him. According to the map Ms Michaelchuk had given him, the cafeteria was on the main floor, south wing.

He headed north instead. The whole morning had been a strain — people reacting to him in unexpected ways, dealing with him according to what he used to be, what they remembered of him. But, hey guys, the thing is, I don't know who you are. Heck, I don't even know who I am. By itself, this was more than enough to give a guy Excedrin headache number three. What kicked it into the red zone on the pain scale was the fact that the few puzzle pieces he had managed to pick up were hinting at a finished picture he wasn't sure he wanted to see.

He wanted out — out into the schoolyard for a little fresh air, and a respite from curious eyes.

He pushed his way through the steel fire door and filled his lungs with the crisp, early-spring air. He caught a gentle floral scent and gazed over to the schoolyard fence. A mauve-hued flowering shrub leaned hard against the chain-link. Lilac, he thought automatically. A small surge of excitement ran through him, the way it always did when he remembered something, and knew without being told that the memory was true.

But the excitement proved fleeting, as another truth settled on him — the truth that the thing he had remembered was not among the things he wanted most desperately to remember. What difference did it make whether the blossoms were lilac or hollyhock or honeysuckle when the only thing he knew about himself was his name?

He glanced around. The schoolyard was deserted. Because the air was still cool, the picnic tables behind the school stood empty. Jack perched on one, his feet on the bench, and opened his lunchbag. His mother had packed an apple, a six-pack of oatmeal cookies, and a sandwich: roast beef, lettuce. He peeked under the top slice of bread and saw something that looked like mustard, except that it was a dull colour, not the vivid yellow stuff they served in the hospital. He let the bread fall back into place and took a tentative bite. It was mustard all right. Spicy mustard. Really hot stuff. He took another bite. Hey, this stuff was really good.

He was finishing the second half of his sandwich when a shadow fell across his feet. He looked up into Mitch Cameron's smiling face.

"I've been looking for you," Mitch said. "I

should have known you'd be out here."

"You should have?" Jack popped the last bit of sandwich into his mouth and wished he had something to drink.

"Sure," Mitch said. He perched on the picnic table beside Jack and pulled a pack of cigarettes from his pocket. He took one for himself and offered the package to Jack. Jack stared at it.

"Do I smoke?" he asked.

Mitch laughed. "It must be weird. You really don't remember much, do you?"

"I don't remember anything," Jack said. He looked at the cigarettes. "So, do I?"

"Do you want to?"

Jack shrugged. "I hear it's not a healthy thing to do."

"Neither is taking on some clown twice your size," Mitch said, "but that never kept you out of a good fight."

Mitch dug into his pocket and pulled out a disposable lighter. He flicked it and lit his cigarette. "Besides, healthy is dull, Jack. Dull and boring and no damn fun at all." He tucked his lighter back into his jacket pocket. "So, I take it you don't want one."

"No, thanks," Jack said.

"No thanks?" Mitch hooted with laughter. "Jeeze, Jack, I can see I'm going to have to work at getting you back into shape."

"Into shape?"

"Back to the good old Jack. The guy I used to know and love." He slapped Jack on the back. "Cheer up, Jackie. You may not remember, but I sure haven't forgotten. Stick with me and you'll be the wild man of Kennedy High again."

The wild man of Kennedy High? Jack felt the pressure of a migraine build up behind his left eye. "How wild?"

Mitch grinned. "Well, that's what we'll have to find out, won't we? And I know just the way to get started. Meet me here after school, Jack. We'll go down to Mario's."

"Mario's?"

"The pool hall."

"I play pool?"

Mitch laughed. "I'd say that's a matter of opinion, Jack." He pushed himself off the picnic table and ground his cigarette butt under the heel of his boot. "I have to go, Jack. Got some business to attend to. Catch you later, okay? Right here. Three-thirty."

Jack nodded and bit into his apple as Mitch disappeared around the side of the school.

7

After the last class of the day, when he stopped at his locker to pick up the books he would need for homework, Jack was assaulted. He was reaching up to the top shelf when suddenly someone thwacked him on the back with a binder.

"Hey!" Jack protested. He spun around and found himself looking into the chocolate eyes of his new lab partner. "What'd you do that for?"

"Why didn't you tell me?" Cleo Taradash said.

"Tell you what?"

"That you were in the hospital and that you almost died. I'm new around here, you know. I can't be expected to know everything. I felt like an idiot when I found out."

Jack studied her. "You mean you had a guilty conscience?" he said at last.

Her nostrils flared. "What do you mean? Why should I feel guilty?"

"Because you treated me like a jerk in chemistry," Jack said.

"I did not."

"Sure you did. You acted like you'd just been stuck with Bozo the Clown for a lab partner."

"Yeah?" Her chin jutted out. She had one hand planted on her hip. "And I suppose you're going to tell me your Einstein's second cousin? Look, I'm sorry I said you looked like Boo Radley, okay? I didn't know you were in a coma for eight months. But I wasn't born yesterday, either. I did my homework. And from what I've heard about you, I sure don't need to apologize for calling you illiterate — "

"Semi-literate, I believe you said."

The distinction seemed to annoy her. "Whatever. You weren't exactly brilliant before your accident, so I don't think we're in grave danger of finding out that you're a genius now. Look, I have a four-point-oh grade-point average and there's no way I'm going to let you screw that up. If Bradley wants you to be my lab partner, there's nothing I can do about it. But I'll do the work, okay? All you have to do is watch. If you want to mess up, wait until next year when you can do it all by yourself. Hey!" She cuffed his arm. "Are you listening to me?"

He hadn't been listening. He had been staring down the hallway at a honey-haired girl. Cleo followed his gaze.

The girl looked at Jack. She froze, like a deer caught in the glare of a car's headlights.

Leah, he thought. He mouthed the word.

The girl's eyes widened. The colour drained from her face. Then, abruptly, she turned and scurried away.

"You're wasting your time," Cleo said.

Jack looked quizzically at her.

"She's taken."

"Taken?"

"Going steady. Has been for months."

Jack stared at the empty hallway where only moments before Leah Bennett had been standing. He thought of mauve ink and the words *Eternally yours*. If she had been going steady with some other guy for several months, then they obviously weren't making eternity the way they used to.

8

"Nice, huh?" Mitch said.

Jack gazed around the pool hall. Mario's looked like a dive right out of one of the fifties videos he had seen in the hospital. In fact, everything reminded him of something out of a video from some era or other, or out of a television program. He had watched a lot of TV after he woke up. Now he found it was one of his main reference points.

"So," Mitch said, nudging Jack in the ribs, "how about you and me shoot a little eight ball?"

"Eight ball?"

"Yeah. To win, what you do is pocket all the balls lower than the eight — or all the higher balls — and then the eight."

Jack looked at the balls on the table. It sounded easy enough.

"Am I high or low?"

"That remains to be seen," Mitch said. "It depends on what you sink first."

Mitch hefted a couple of cues from a rack on the wall and tossed one to Jack.

"You want to break?" Mitch asked.

"Break?"

"That white ball is the cue ball," Mitch explained in a friendly voice. "Relax, Jack. Take your time. Line up the cue ball and send it right on through. Not too soft, not too hard. Just right on through."

His voice was soft, encouraging. Jack relaxed under its soothing spell and bent to the task at hand. He pulled his cue back, not too far, and stared down its sleek length as if he were a marksman in a western movie. He eased forward, swinging, striking the cue ball, sending it careering forward, forward . . . and only kissing the first of the balls in the triangle, dislodging it and its mates only slightly. Red-faced, Jack looked back up at Mitch.

Mitch grinned. "Some things never change, huh? Maybe you should get a paper and pencil, Jack. Maybe you should take notes, because the master is going to show you a few tricks."

Mitch lined up the cue ball and fired it against the six, which ricocheted off one of the sides and dropped with a click into a side pocket.

"So, Jack," he said as he studied the lay of the table for a moment, "what's it like?" He swung his arm back, then forward in one fluid movement. The cue ball nudged the two into a corner pocket. "You really don't remember anything?"

"Not a thing," Jack said.

The smile faded from Mitch's face. He studied Jack a moment. "What's it like?"

It? "The amnesia?"

"Yeah."

"It's . . . a little unsettling."

"Unsettling?" Mitch roared with laughter. "Jeeze, Jack, you sound like a different person."

I feel like a different person, Jack thought.

"Is your memory ever going to come back?"

That was the million-dollar question. Answer it correctly, Dr. Bunny, and you'll win . . . the undying gratitude of one totally weirded-out Jack Thorne.

"I . . . they . . . my doctor doesn't know. Maybe."

"And maybe not?"

Jack nodded slowly. That was the scary part. The maybe not. But it's not the end of the world, Bugs had told him. It's not any worse than . . . well, than any other slight disability. Jack liked that. Slight. Like being blind or deaf or mute. Real slight.

"That's tough," Mitch said. He lined up another shot and sank the three. "But, hey, that doesn't mean things can't be the way they used to be." He slapped Jack on the back as he circled the table to set up another shot. "Anything you can't remember, I'll fill in the blanks, okay?" He drew aim on the one ball, and missed. "Your turn."

"Thanks," Jack said. He studied the table and headed for the far end.

"You're better over here," Mitch said. "Nine in the left corner."

Jack checked the nine ball. Mitch was right. It could be one he might make.

"Just concentrate, Jackie." Mitch's voice washed over him like a warm wave. He focused all his energy on the nine. "The stick is just an extension of your arm. You're part of it."

Jack drew his arm back.

"That's it, Jackie, slow and smooth, not too soft now, not too hard."

The cue ball rolled toward the nine and hit it. The nine sailed into the left corner pocket and disappeared from sight.

"You got it, Jackie!" Mitch said. "The power of concentration!"

Jack smiled and couldn't remember the last time he had done that. He studied the lay of the table and began to set up his next shot. He glanced up at Mitch, who nodded.

"That's the one I'd go for," he said.

"Mitch!"

Jack looked across the room. Three guys in leather jackets were staring at him. The one in the middle, the tallest one, had called.

"Hey, Gary," Mitch answered. He set his cue into the rack. "Go for it, man," he said to Jack. "I'll be right back."

Jack tried the shot . . . and missed. He stood beside the table and watched Mitch, Gary, and the other two guys. Gary looked angry about something. He poked Mitch sharply with an index finger while he talked, and glanced pointedly at Jack a couple of times. Mitch wore his habitual grin when he loped back to Jack a few minutes later, but somehow the grin clashed with the look in his eyes.

"Problem?" Jack asked,

"Problem?" Mitch reached for his stick. His back was turned to Jack. "There's no problem. Hell, Gary and me are pals. We go way back."

Mitch attacked the table with laser-pointed determination and cleared it of low balls in short order. Then he sank the eight.

"Rack 'em up, Jack," he said. "Let's play again."

THREE

1

His mother was waiting for him. She must have watched him come up the walk, because the door opened even before he had a chance to try the handle.

"How was your day?" she asked. The words were right out of a *Leave It To Beaver* re-run, perky old June in her pearls and her high heels, greeting her menfolk as they returned to the nest. But her eyes held none of June's eternal optimism. She looked worried. "Did everything go okay? Why are you so late getting home? Oh, Jack, I was so worried. I thought maybe something had happened."

She didn't say what, and he couldn't bring himself to ask. He was afraid the question would unleash another torrent of tears. But he couldn't help wondering what she thought could have happened.

"I'm fine," he said. "I stopped off to play some pool with Mitch."

She looked surprised. "You played pool with Mitch? Mitch Cameron?"

Jack nodded, but her startled look threw him off balance.

"He said he and I used to be friends. We were friends, weren't we?"

"Well, yes, you were friends," she said reluctantly. "It's just that I'm not sure I think it's such a very good idea."

"Who thinks what's not a very good idea?" John Thorne came out of the study carrying an attache case and consulting the gold Rolex on his wrist.

"N-nothing," Jack's mother said quickly. She glanced at Jack. "I was just wondering if it was such a good idea for Jack to go to school today. He looks so tired."

"He looks fine to me." Jack's father barely glanced at him. "I have to run if I'm going to catch that plane." He planted a perfunctory kiss on his wife's cheek. "See you tomorrow night."

"John, I wish you'd stay home."

"For heaven's sake, Elise, we've been over that a hundred times. I have to go. This is a very important meeting." He glanced at his watch again. "I have to run."

His mother's lips trembled as she watched her husband leave, and the door close quietly behind him.

"I'm sorry I was late," Jack said. Just please don't cry, he begged silently. He didn't know what it was about her tears that got to him, but he would do almost anything to prevent them. The trouble was, it was next to impossible to tell what brought them on. It made conversation with his mother like a game of Russian roulette. "I should have phoned you."

Her eyes brimmed. Do something, Jack. Change the subject. Divert the flood. Say something. He said the first thing that came to his mind. "I'm starving. I hope I didn't miss dinner."

Bingo. He had hit the maternal instinct button dead on. She smiled immediately.

"It's Marguerite's day off. But she left some fried chicken."

It sounded good. But then, Jack realized, raw chicken would have sounded good. It had been an awfully long time since lunch, and he had been more active today than he had been for as long as he could remember.

He followed his mother into the kitchen where she had laid two places at a small pine table in the corner. She served him happily, and he ate with equal gusto — fried chicken, potato salad, devilled eggs, and heavy brown bread that defied description.

"It's so good," he said.

"Marguerite made it especially for you. It was one of your favourites when you were little."

"Marguerite is a good cook," he said as he buttered another thick slice.

"Well," his mother said slowly when he finally pushed himself away from the table, "I suppose you'll be wanting to get to your homework." She looked so sad that Jack shook his head.

"From what I've been able to figure out, another few minutes away from the books isn't going to affect my standing one way or the other." He smiled gently at her. "Why didn't you tell me I wasn't a good student?"

She looked so aggrieved that he regretted the question almost as soon as he had asked it.

"I — " She looked down at her lap where her hands picked nervously at the hem of her apron. "I guess I didn't think it would help you to know. Besides, you weren't such a bad student."

Mothers. Maybe Bugs was right about them. Maybe it was true: "The way it works, Jack, is that your mother always loves you. Your mother always sees you in a way no one else does." He had entered seven classrooms today and had read the eyes of seven teachers, and in none of them had he seen the optimism he now saw in his mother's eyes.

"I found some old test papers upstairs," he

said. "It looks like on a good day I was making D-minus."

His mother winced. "When you were little, you were so clever," she said. Her voice trembled. "It was just recently, Jack. Just in the year before the . . . the accident."

Jack didn't understand. "What was in the year before the accident?"

A tear slipped down one cheek. "I don't know what happened," she said. "I should have known. If I was a good mother, I would have known. But I didn't, Jack."

Jack wished he could reach across the table and wipe the tear from her cheek, but something held him back.

"Don't cry," he said softly.

"You were just . . . different, that's all. You didn't tell me why. You . . . you just stopped talking to me, Jack." Her tears were flowing freely now. He sat in helpless silence while she battled them, her napkin-wrapped hand darting here and there, capturing this one and that, until finally they were all gone.

"Well," she said, rising briskly and starting to clear the table, "you have your homework."

It was an opportunity to escape, but he didn't take it. "What was I like when I was a kid?" he asked.

A smile graced her lips again. "You were such a sweet little boy," she said. She set the dishes into the sink and wiped her hands on a tea towel. "Do you want to see some pictures?"

"Sure," Jack said. "I'd like that."

She had a dozen thick albums, and settled in to guide him through each one.

"This is you when you were newborn," she said. "You were so beautiful. The most beautiful baby I've ever seen, and I'm not just saying that because I'm your mother."

Jack peered at the scrunch-faced bald-headed infant with the little pug nose, and saw nothing even remotely attractive. He couldn't believe that had once been him.

"And this is you when I had you baptised," she said. "You see that dress you're wearing? That was worn by my father when he was baptised."

"Where does he live?"

Her eyes clouded. "Your grandfather died a long time ago," she said softly. Then she turned the page of the album and her face brightened. "Oh, your first birthday! I remember it as if it were yesterday . . . "

She led him through the pages, through a life that he didn't remember at all, that might as well have belonged to a complete stranger.

Then he noticed it. "Why aren't there any pictures of . . . of my father?" Or maybe he should have said Dad. Or, surely not, Daddy?

His mother looked vaguely uncomfortable. "If you mean John," she said, "he wasn't around then. Oh, look! This is you when you won the fourth grade science fair. I was so proud — "

"What do you mean, 'If I mean John?' Who else would I mean?"

His mother's smile was distant, almost full of longing. "Your real father died before you were born, Jack. I only have one picture of him." She got up and burrowed in the bottom drawer of her desk. When she came back to sit beside him, she had a small box in her hand. She opened it and took out a wallet-size black and white photograph. "That's him. That's your real father. It's funny, he wasn't much older than you are now, Jack, when he died."

Jack stared at the photograph of the serious-looking young man in military garb and a marine-style haircut. He handed it back to his mother, and saw the love and longing in her eyes as she slipped it back into the box.

"You look so much like him," she said. "You are so much like him."

"So John Thorne is . . ."

"He's your father, too, Jack. He adopted you when we got married. You were ten years old."

John Thorne wasn't his father. Not his real father.

"Oh, look, this is you that summer you went to camp."

Jack looked at the picture. But his thoughts were on John Thorne.

2

Jack sat at his desk and stared at his chemistry
text. He tried to study, but found it was like
trying to read Greek when he had never been
introduced to the language. No wonder I didn't
do well at this, he thought with despair. It doesn't
make any sense.

Nor was it easy to study when his mind kept
wandering. He kept staring at the photograph
tucked into the corner of his mirror.

"What about Leah Bennett?" he had asked
his mother.

"Leah Bennett?" She was so flustered by the
mention of the name that she lost her grip on the
photograph album on her lap. It slid with a
thump to the floor.

"Her picture is in my mirror upstairs."

His mother busied herself with picking up
the album and flipping through its pages until
she found her place.

"Did you see her at school today?" She struggled to sound casual, but Jack detected a quaver
in her voice and a blush in her cheeks.

Jack nodded.

"Did she . . . did she say anything to you?"

"About what?"

His mother fussed with a photograph that
had slipped sideways under its protective glas-
sine sheet. "Well, I don't know," she said without

looking at him. Without daring to look at him, Jack thought. She fiddled with another photograph. "I just thought she might have said something."

"She looked at me as if she had seen a ghost," Jack said. "She didn't say anything at all." Was that relief that he saw in his mother's eyes? "Why do you think she did that?"

"Well, I don't know," his mother said. "It's been a long time since she's seen you and . . . well, I'm sure things have changed for her."

Unless Leah had been in the habit of jack-rabbiting from him in the days when she was "eternally" his, things had definitely changed. Besides, Cleo Taradash had told him that Leah had been dating someone else for months.

Forget about her, he told himself. His mother was right. Things had changed. Things had changed a lot.

He stood up abruptly, grabbed the photograph from the corner of his mirror, and stared angrily at it. *Eternally yours,* she had written. Or until you have a nasty accident, whichever comes first. He held the picture in both hands, and ripped it in half. So much for eternity.

He sat back down again and forced himself to read the words in his chemistry text aloud. It didn't do any good. He still couldn't make sense of them. Angrily he slammed his book shut. What was the point anyway? He was a crummy student, and everyone knew it, with the possible exception of his mother. He had been pulling Ds and Fs, for pete's sake. It wasn't as if a caved-in skull was going to suddenly transform him into a genius. He rolled his desk chair over to the computer table in the corner of his room.

If he had ever known anything about computers, he had long since forgotten it. And he was probably too stupid to learn it again, he thought sourly.

What kind of life had he managed to drop into? Who was this guy Jack Thorne? Someone who knew how to throw a punch but not how to solve a simple equation. A guy whose mother drank a little too much and cried way too much. A father — no, excuse me, make that a step-father — who didn't seem too thrilled to have him back from never-never land. A guy whose girlfriend — oops, another slip, make that ex-girlfriend — turned and ran in the opposite direction the first time she saw him.

Just about the only person who didn't act weird around him, who didn't treat him like he was a freak, thought Jack, was Mitch. Mitch didn't think he was a lunatic just because he couldn't remember his favourite flavour of ice-cream. Mitch seemed supremely confident that Jack could learn whatever he had forgotten. Like how to shoot pool. Or how to use a computer. Jack wished he shared that confidence.

He must know — better make that must have known — something about computers. He had one, didn't he? He flipped open the lid of the diskette holder beside the computer. It held games. Lots of them. *Frogger* and *Space Invaders, Bouncing Babies, Janitor Joe, The Butler* and *The Wizard*. And in the back of the case, a couple of diskettes labeled History, Homework, English. And one disk that had no label at all.

He had done his homework on the computer, which said something about how hard the thing must be to operate. Although he was pulling down Fs and Ds, he had at least been smart enough to do his homework on a computer.

Well, if he could learn to play pool — okay, if he could make a start at learning to play pool — he could sure learn to handle a computer.

Maybe.

The first thing he had to do was turn the machine on. How hard could that be?

It took him a few minutes to locate the switch. He flipped it up. The machine hummed softly, but nothing happened on the screen.

Damn.

Then he noticed what looked to be a small light in the corner of the monitor frame. The light was off. He hunted around under the frame, found a switch, and flipped it. Letters appeared on the screen.

Okay. He had it up and running. Now what?

And what the heck did that mean, anyway, that
C: on the screen?

He glanced at the small bookshelf above the
computer table and found a manual. If he wanted
to go any further than this, he was going to have
to study up on the machine. Jack sighed. Maybe
it would turn out he was a computer genius.
Maybe that was his redeeming talent. He pulled
the manual from the shelf and settled back in his
chair to read it.

Two hours had passed by the time he had the
program loaded and had figured out how to read
his data disks.

The homework disks were depressing. He
remembered little of the subjects they covered,
and learned less from reading the essays he had
written. It wasn't hard to see why his grade point
average was as low as it was.

Then he took the unlabelled disk and slipped
it into the disk drive. But when he tried to call
up its menu, only a line of text appeared at the
bottom of the screen. INCOMPATIBLE FILE FOR-
MAT, it stated.

He flipped back and forth through the
manual for a few minutes trying to find out what
was wrong, but found nothing. Besides, it was
late and he was tired. It had been a long day.

Cleo barely glanced at him when he set his books down onto the marble top of the lab bench the next morning. She plunked a test tube down into a test tube rack.

"Glad you could make it," she said sourly.

Jack glanced at his watch, then at the clock above the door. "I'm three minutes early," he said.

Cleo stabbed a test tube into the last vacant slot, and eyed him disparagingly.

"This is a complicated experiment," she said. "If we're not set up and ready to go the minute the bell rings, we'll be back here again after school to finish up. I don't know about you, but I have better things to do this afternoon."

When Jack said nothing, she ducked down under the counter and produced two beakers and a bunsen burner.

"Get the sodium dichloride," she said.

Jack stared blankly at her, but she was busy measuring droppersful of a clear liquid into each test tube. It was a moment before she looked up at him and said impatiently, "Well? What are you waiting for? Hell to freeze over?"

"Actually," Jack said, "I was waiting for you to tell me where to find the . . . whatchamacall-it."

"The sodium dichloride," Cleo said. She rolled her eyes. "Did you read the experiment?

Do you even know what we're trying to accomplish here?"

"Well, not exactly," Jack admitted.

Cleo's eyes bugged out of her head. "You didn't even read the experiment? No wonder you were just barely scraping through! You must have been one of those guys everyone gave a D to just to get rid of them — " She turned away from him in disgust and pulled open a cupboard. It was filled with rows of neatly-labelled bottles. She waved one under his nose. "This is sodium dichloride," she said.

"I can read," he said evenly. "All you had to do was tell me which cupboard."

"All you had to do was read the experiment."

"I did."

"But you said — "

"I read the experiment. What I meant was, I don't understand what we're trying to accomplish here."

"Are you trying to be funny?"

"No."

"Well, if you read the experiment, it should be obvious."

"It might be obvious to you. But it isn't to me. Look, if you really don't want me for a lab partner, I can get Mr. Bradley to re-assign me."

"I wish you would," she muttered.

"Fine." Maybe Bradley would pair him with the class idiot. That was probably where he belonged. "No problem." He gathered his books and headed for the front of the class.

"Hey, wait!" she called. "Come on, Jack."

He turned slowly and was surprised to see how completely the anger had disappeared from her face.

"I'm sorry," she said. "I did it again. Acted like a real jerk. I don't know what gets into me sometimes. It's just that I want to do well, you know? It's important to me."

"I thought you were doing well."

A blush crept into her cheeks. "Well, I am. But I want to do better than that. I'm going for a scholarship."

"Oh. You mean you want to be the best."

The gentle roses in her cheeks turned to flashpoints of anger. "What's wrong with that? Look, maybe you don't have to worry about who's going to finance your education. You live on the Hill, don't you? In one of those big houses. Well, I don't. So if I want to get into medical school — "

"Medical school?" That was an interesting twist. Jack imagined her at a bedside, berating a patient.

"That's right. Medical school. And there's only one way I can get there. On a scholarship. So you bet I want to be the best. It's the best or nothing at all for me."

Jack studied the defiant tilt of her chin and the passion that burned in her eyes. "In that case," he said, "you definitely don't need me for a lab partner. From what I've been able to figure out, mediocre would be a big step up for me."

She looked surprised for a minute. "I guess missing a year of school doesn't help much." Then she sighed. "So maybe you aren't the greatest as a lab partner. But I sure could use a good lab assistant. And who knows? Maybe you'll learn something."

By the end of the lab period, he was sure that he had. Once she calmed down, Cleo gave him clear directions and explained every step of the experiment with such enthusiasm that Jack couldn't help sharing her excitement.

"That was fun," he said as he cleaned up the last of the test tubes while Cleo wrote up the results. As he dried the beaker, he noticed that most of the other teams in the lab were only halfway through their experiments. When the bell finally rang, he and Cleo were the only ones not to groan.

Cleo slapped her notebook shut and grinned at him. "Glad you enjoyed it," she said. "Maybe there's hope for you yet."

Jack grinned. "I like to think so," he said, gathering his texts. "Where's your next class?"

"Third floor."

Jack's smile widened. "Mine, too," he said. "Mind if I walk with you?"

Her smile was as enigmatic as the Mona

Lisa's. "No, I guess not." She walked beside him in silence for a moment. He could feel her looking at him. "Jack, can I ask you a question?"

"Sure, I guess."

"What happened to you? I mean, I heard you were in the hospital for a long time . . . "

"I don't know," Jack said.

Like a match just struck, her anger blazed. "Look, if you don't want to tell me — "

"I'd love to tell you. The truth is, I don't remember."

"Don't remember?"

"I was in an accident. A car accident. At least, that's what I've been told. Apparently I totalled my old man's car three days after I got my driver's license."

"And?"

"And," Jack said, "that's all I know. I don't remember anything that happened to me before I woke up in the hospital."

Her eyes were incredulous as she gazed up at him. She opened her mouth to speak, but someone else called his name first. Called it shrilly, from far down the corridor. Jack turned and saw a woman hurrying toward him.

"Jack! Jack Thorne! I heard you were back. I heard you were here."

The woman's dark, uncombed hair was heavily salted with grey. It flew around her head as she ran to him.

"Where is he, Jack? Where did he go? He must have told you something."

Her eyes were wild and crazy. She clutched Jack's arm and held it tightly.

"Please, Jack. Just tell me where he is. Tell me!"

Jack glanced helplessly at Cleo, who seemed as alarmed at the woman's behaviour as he was himself.

"Please, Jack. You and Ed were such good friends. You and Ed and Mitch. You were like the Three Musketeers."

Jack tried to pull away from the woman. "Please, lady. I don't know what you're talking about." But the woman clung more tightly. Tears gathered in her eyes as she begged him to tell her something, anything, about a person whose name Jack didn't even recognize.

A crowd gathered around Jack and Cleo and the woman. A hundred pairs of eyes watched the woman plead and cry until, finally, Mr. Morris pushed his way through the crowd and detached her from Jack quickly and efficiently.

"Now, Mrs. Lyle," he said as he escorted the sobbing woman through the crowd, "I don't think this is accomplishing anything at all. The boy doesn't remember . . . "

Jack realized that he was trembling. He stood beside Cleo in the hallway, his heart pounding, his throat dry, wondering what the woman wanted from him. Cleo eyed him disparagingly and shook her head.

"Mitch?" she said. "Mitch Cameron?"

Jack nodded.

"You were friends with Mitch Cameron?"

Jack nodded again.

Cleo sighed. "You must have been a bigger jerk than I thought," she said. She shook her head again. "Come on. We're going to be late for class."

4

"Ed? You mean, Ed Lyle?" Mitch held a match to the end of his cigarette. "Of course I know him. Why? What about him?"

"Did something happen to him?" Jack said.

"You mean about him taking off the way he did?"

"He took off?"

"Ran away. I know the guy was your friend, Jack. Hell, I guess he was my friend, too, although you and him were the closest. But Ed had problems. A lot of problems. He was always running around trying to be super reporter, when he couldn't even get assigned a real article on the school newspaper. He made a complete fool of himself a couple of times trying to get the big story, and always acting like he was onto something as hot as Watergate. One time he wrote this article on payola on the school radio station. Can you beat that? The only way the station can afford to stay on the air is if they get records donated from the record companies, and old Ed's making a big deal of it, calling it payola. Everyone was laughing at him. And then there was his home situation."

"What about his home situation?"

"It was depressing, that's what about it." Mitch shook his head suddenly, as if to clear it. "I have to tell you, Jack, this whole thing is really messing up my head. I mean, here you are, sitting out here with me, you look like the same old Jack." He shrugged. "Okay, so maybe you're a few kilos off your peak weight, and a little sun wouldn't hurt you. But basically you look like the same old Jack. I keep expecting you to sound like the same old Jack. I keep forgetting, you know?"

Jack smiled wryly. "Yeah. I know." When it came to forgetting, Jack was the expert. "So what about Ed's home life?"

"Ed's father dumped his mother. For his secretary, if you can believe it. Classic case, huh? Anyway, the way Ed told it, his mother went nuts. She'd get crazy every time Ed left the house. She used to call everyone in the neighbourhood if he was five minutes late. It was like now she had lost her husband, she was terrified she was going to lose Ed. She made his life such hell that she really did lose him. Ironic, huh?" He peered at Jack a moment. "You're asking a lot of questions about a guy you don't even remember, Jack. Time for me to ask one. Why the big interest in Ed Lyle?"

"A woman . . . his mother . . . seems to think I might know where he is."

"You talked to Mildred?"

"She was here at school. She grabbed me and started asking me if I knew where Ed was. Do I?"

Mitch shrugged. "You tell me."

"Mrs. Morris says Ed Lyle disappeared about the same time I had my accident."

Mitch dragged thoughtfully on his cigarette. "Yeah," he said, "now that you mention it, I guess that's right. I hadn't given it much thought. To tell you the truth, Jack, I was more worried about what had happened to you. About whether you were going to make it." He smiled. "I'm glad you did."

Jack returned the smile. Maybe he didn't remember Mitch. But he didn't need his memory to figure out why he and Mitch had been friends. Mitch was so relaxed, so easy to like.

"Don't you know where he is?"

"He never told me where he was going, no."

"So nobody knows where he is?"

Mitch grinned. "There's always somebody who knows, Jack. I guess the people where Ed is now know where he is, if you get my meaning. It's just Mildred who doesn't know. Let me tell you something, Jack. She just doesn't get it. She can't take a hint, you know? She had the cops looking for him for a while. Then she hired a P.I. She just refuses to accept that Ed took off on account of her."

"He's never contacted her?"

"Not that I know of." Mitch took a last drag on his cigarette, then stubbed it out. "If he'd told anyone where he was going, I guess he would have told you. Ironic, huh, Jack? He's probably wondering how come you forgot to write. Get it? Forgot to write."

Mitch's smile faded when Jack's failed to materialize. It was replaced with a sheepish grin.

"Jeeze, I'm sorry Jack," he said. "I didn't mean anything by that. Just a little humour, you know? A little comic relief." He perched again on the picnic table beside Jack. "I don't know where Ed went. But wherever he is, I hope he's having one hell of a good time. Poor guy deserves it after what he went through with Mildred." He nudged Jack. "Hey, you want to shoot some pool later?"

Pool. Time away from the discomfort of home. Time with Mitch, who was the only person besides Bugs who made Jack feel relaxed.

"Yeah," Jack said. "Yeah, I'd like to."

Jack looped the lock back through the handle of his locker, tucked his stack of homework books under his arm, rounded the corner, and ran smack into her.

Her books clattered to the floor, but she made no move to retrieve them. Instead, she stood deathly still in the hallway and stared at him through shock-widened eyes.

Jack stooped and gathered her books for her. "I'm sorry," he said. "I didn't mean to startle you."

It was as if his voice triggered something in her. She grabbed her books from him and started to scuttle away backward.

"Leah!" he called. "Leah, wait. Please."

She came to a stop and stared at him, her pale blue eyes watery. She clung to her books and binders as if they were a life raft. Close up, she was even more beautiful than she had appeared in the photograph in Jack's mirror. But her eyes weren't smiling. She looked as scared as she had that first time — well, the first time he could remember — he had seen her.

"I don't bite," he said softly.

"Jack, I-I . . ."

"Leah?" a voice called.

Jack turned with her to see a muscular guy striding toward them. He looked like grade-A linebacker material.

"Leah?" he said, his voice a low rumble, like a mine threatening to cave in. "Is this guy bothering you?"

"N-no, Todd," Leah said quickly. She clutched her books to her chest and hurried to him. "I was just . . . I just dropped my books, and . . . "

Todd eyed Jack menacingly. "I know who you are. You're that guy who was in a coma, right?" He didn't look at all pleased that Jack had awakened.

Jack stared mutely at the mountain named Todd. Todd hadn't recognized him instantly, which could only mean one thing.

"You're new around here, right?"

Todd stiffened as if he had been challenged. "Yeah. So?"

"Todd." She made the word sound like a plea. Her eyes joined in the effort.

"So nothing," Jack said. "Leah and I used to know each other. I just wanted to talk to her. For old time's sake." He looked at Leah. Her eyes were wide as she stared at him, her chin sagged a little, like someone who is just a little afraid. But afraid of what? She must have cared for him at some time. She had signed her picture *Eternally*. Or had she signed a dozen other pictures the same way for a dozen other guys? He suddenly realized that he had no way of knowing.

"Yeah," Todd said. "I heard you used to know each other. But you don't know each other any more, pal, so why don't you just run along?"

"Todd, it's okay," Leah said. She regarded Jack with uneasy eyes.

"No, it's not okay." Todd threw an arm around her and pulled her closer to him. "Look, pal," he said to Jack, "maybe you don't remember what happened, and maybe you do . . . "

I wish, Jack thought.

" . . . but I'm here to tell you that it's over between you and Leah. Finished. She's my girlfriend now and we both like it that way, don't we, Leah?"

Leah nodded. She didn't look at Jack.

"And if I ever catch you bothering her again . . . "

"I wasn't trying to bother her."

Todd squinted through small eyes. "Maybe you used to be something special around here, pal, but that was a long time ago. You try anything with Leah, and you'll have me to deal with."

Jack stared at Leah, whose eyes now filled with tears.

"Now look what you've done," Todd said contemptuously. "Come on, Leah, let's go."

Leah said nothing, but allowed herself to be led away. As Jack watched her go, someone behind him said, "She never was worth the trouble, if you ask me."

Jack whirled around to face Mitch. His

cheeks grew hot as he realized Mitch had seen what had happened.

"Hey, I didn't mean to eavesdrop," Mitch said. "I couldn't help it. I was standing right over there." He gestured toward the exit door behind Jack. "Having a smoke, you know?"

"Yeah." Jack turned and looked down the hallway. Leah was gone.

Mitch smiled sympathetically and slapped Jack lightly on the shoulder.

"Come on, Jackie. I'll stand you to a cold drink. Then I'll beat your ass at the pool table. How about it?" His grin was mischievous.

Thank God for Mitch, Jack thought, the one person in the world who doesn't make me feel like a freak.

"Yeah," Jack said. "Yeah, okay. Let's go to Mario's."

"No, not Mario's," Mitch said quickly. "Frank's."

"Frank's?"

"Another place I know."

Another place. He made it sound special. In fact, it looked exactly like Mario's except that it had a dozen tables. Mario's only had eight.

"Rack 'em up," Mitch said. "I'll choose our weapons."

Jack arranged the balls on the table and watched Mitch select first one cue, then a second.

"You break," Mitch said.

Jack obliged. His break was wild, scattering the balls all over the table, and even he, with his limited knowledge of the game, could see how well he had set Mitch up.

"What did you mean," he asked while Mitch studied his play, "when you said she wasn't worth the trouble?"

Mitch winked at him. "Babes are never worth the trouble."

"Yeah, but when you said it about Leah, it sounded like you had something specific in mind."

Mitch leaned over the table, hinged his arm back and slid the cue ball into the nine, which slipped easily into the corner pocket. He reached for the chalk while he decided on his next play.

"So, what did you mean?"

Mitch looked away from the table with a sigh. "Look, I'm sorry I opened my big mouth, okay? Let's just forget I said anything. Let's have a good time." He circled the table and bent to his next shot. Jack circled to meet him, and clapped a hand firmly on Mitch's cue.

"What did you mean?"

Mitch wrenched his cue free. "Jeeze," he said, "some things never change. You're the same pain in the butt you used to be. Always asking questions when anyone in his right mind wouldn't want to know the answers." He studied Jack a minute, and sighed again. "Okay," he said. "But what's the point? It was a long time ago. Hell, if you can't remember bad things, you should be glad. You shouldn't go around begging people to remind you."

"What do you mean, bad?"

Mitch shook his head. "You're not going to leave this alone, are you, Jack? Okay. I just meant that after . . . the accident, well, I would have thought she'd care a little more, that's all. After all, you two went together for almost a year."

A year. A long time.

"I just thought . . . I thought she might have waited a little longer before she started going out with the Moose — "

"Moose? You mean, Todd?"

"Yeah. I mean, if she was my girl and the minute I landed in the hospital she started seeing some other guy, well, I guess I'd wonder about how much she really cared about me in the first place, you know, and how much she was just stringing me along. I'm sorry, Jack. Like I said, I should have kept my mouth shut. I'm sorry I said anything at all."

As Mitch bent over the table, a lump formed in Jack's throat. Go with your instincts, Bugs was always telling him. Never mind who you used to be. You are, that's the important thing. And the way you can learn about who you really are is to go with your instincts. Well, damn it, he should have gone with his instincts. He should have known that whoever he was, he wasn't a guy who could hold the interest of a girl like Leah Bennett.

The list of failures from his previous life kept growing. He was a poor student. He was a lousy pool player. His girlfriend threw him over the minute he landed in the hospital. . . .

"Mitch!"

Mitch straightened slowly. His face was grim as he turned to greet Gary. The smile that spread slowly across his face was taut and dangerous.

"Hi, Gary. I didn't expect to see you here."

"Yeah," Gary said drily. "I bet you didn't." He approached their table slowly, flanked by the same two gorillas who had been with him a couple of days ago in Mario's. His slate-grey eyes slithered over Jack like a couple of snakes. "Hi there, Jack."

Jack glanced at Mitch, who eyed Gary with outright hostility, then looked back at Gary.

"I hear you're not great with names these days, so let me make it easy for you. I'm Gary. This is Len, and that's Pete."

Neither Len nor Pete acknowledged Jack. They hung behind Gary, one on each side, like two bodyguards.

"What do you want, Gary?" Mitch asked in a flat tone.

"Hey, take it easy, Mitch. I just want to welcome Jack back to the neighbourhood. Nothing wrong with wanting to be friendly, is there?" He flashed Jack a smile that was all ice.

"I'm sure Jack appreciates the gesture," Mitch said. "Now if you don't mind . . . "

Gary's grey eyes narrowed. "You should relax, Mitch. You can't play a good game when you're so tense." He stood patiently, waiting Mitch out. Finally Mitch bent over the table and made his shot.

"Do we know each other?" Jack asked.

Gary's gaze was cool. "Know each other? Sure we know each other. We got acquainted before your little . . . accident."

Jack didn't like the spin he put on the last word.

"So, where are you staying now, Jack?" Gary asked. The question seemed casual enough, but Gary's eyes were studying him the way a lion studies its prey.

"Staying?" It was a peculiar question. "You mean, where do I live?"

Gary's smile spread like an oil slick. "Yeah, where you live. That's what I mean."

Jack glanced at Mitch, who now seemed immersed in studying his next shot.

"I live at home."

"At home?" He sounded genuinely surprised, but the surprise was not reflected in his eyes. "You're not living with your folks, are you?"

Mitch straightened up. "Leave him alone, Gary."

Gary's eyes narrowed like gun battlements. "Hey, I'm not bothering him. Jack, am I bothering you?"

Jack shook his head. But Gary *was* bothering him. He was bothering him plenty. "What's wrong with living at home?"

Mitch slammed his pool cue down onto the table. "That's it! Come on, Jack. Let's get out of here."

But it was too late. Jack couldn't walk away. "What's wrong with living with my parents?"

"Come on, Jackie." Mitch pulled on his arm. Jack jerked free of him.

Gary leaned back against the table, his arms crossed over his chest, and smiled.

"Hey, I didn't say there was anything wrong with it, did I? But if my old man and my old lady had hired a lawyer to get them to pull the plug on me, I wouldn't be in a big hurry to live under the same roof with them again. Would you, Mitch?"

Mitch's hands curled into fists at his sides. "Shut up, Gary."

"What are you talking about?" Jack asked.

Gary shook his head slowly. "I hate to be the one to tell you this, Jack. But it seems your folks couldn't keep up with the medical bills. Or maybe they got tired of going down there to see you every day. My son the broccoli, and he's costing us a fortune. I don't know for sure. But I do know that your old man hired a lawyer to draw up the papers, and I do know that they went to court. Hey, who knows, if you hadn't woken up when you did, they might have won it on appeal and then it would have been goodnight, Jack. Permanently."

All feeling drained slowly from Jack's body.

6

He didn't remember going home. He only remembered being there, letting himself into the house and finding his mother in the living room, alone, a glass on the table in front of her. When she looked up at him with bleary eyes, he guessed that she was probably working on a refill.

"Jack!" she said. "You're so late. I was worried."

Worried? She had the gall to say she was worried? He advanced on her like an army cranked up for battle. "Is it true?" he demanded.

Her eyes tightened. She struggled up from her chair, her glass in her hand.

"Jack, why don't you come into the kitchen? I'll have Marguerite fix you something to eat."

"I don't want anything to eat. I want to know if it's true. Did you and . . . John Thorne try to get them to pull the plug on me?"

The glass fell from her hand and shattered on the floor.

"Jack, I don't know who told you that, but —"

"Is it true?" he shouted at her. Shouted so hard that the muscles in his throat seared. So loud that Marguerite, coming into the room with a tray of fresh glasses, started, and the glasses rattled together.

His mother's lips quivered. Her eyes, locked onto his, filled with tears. "Jack, I'm so sorry. I didn't want you to suffer. . . . "

"So you tried to have me killed?" He hated her. He hated her for having wanted to be rid of him, for having tried to be rid of him — and for not having succeeded.

"Jack, I'm sorry." She wept bitterly. Marguerite ran to her, but Jack got to her first and grabbed her by the shoulders. He was surprised how fragile her bones seemed, how delicate, as he shook her.

"You tried to kill me!" It filled his head like a scream. "You tried to kill me!" And everybody knew about it. Mitch and Gary and Len and Pete and God knew who else. They all knew. And if they knew, probably others did, too. Step right up, folks, here he is, the guy whose parents cared about him so much they arranged to have him put to death.

A woman screamed. At first he thought it was his mother. But it couldn't have been, because she had already gone limp in his arms. It was Marguerite screaming. And still he didn't stop shaking his mother, he couldn't stop. He shook and shook and shook, and was only dimly aware of the door crashing open behind him, only faintly aware of the hands that fell on him. Then, abruptly, he was hurled backward. Like a ragdoll thrown against a wall, his entire body made contact at the same time. He shattered, and the world went black around him.

FOUR

*A man's real possession is his memory.
In nothing else is he rich, in nothing
else is he poor.*
> Alexander Smith
> "Of Death and the Fear of
> Dying"
> *Dreamthorp*

1

Jack's eyes fluttered open but didn't focus. Couldn't focus. Not when he was three metres below the surface peering up through almost opaque blackness. He tried to kick his feet, flail his arms, propel himself upwards through the darkness toward the light, but his legs were leaden, he couldn't move them. He couldn't move his arms, either, but he could feel them, straining, wrenching.

He heard a roar, like thunderous waves crashing on a rocky shore. He stopped struggling and strained to listen. The sounds he now heard were muffled, indistinct, like a rumble deep within a cave, so at first he thought he was just

His stomach heaved and churned.

"Ja-a-a-ack?"

He squeezed his eyes shut and clenched his jaw to keep the nausea from sweeping over him. Hold onto it. Don't let it go, Jack, don't let it go.

When his eyes fluttered open again, he was blinded by the light. Automatically he raised an arm to shield his eyes. Or, rather, tried to raise an arm. It wouldn't move. He rolled his head to one side and squinted into the brightness. His hand was tied, for pete's sake. It was wrapped in foam and tied to . . . to the side of the bed. Damn. Both his hands were tied to the bed. Someone must have come at him in his sleep and tied him down and now here he was, trussed like a Thanksgiving turkey, helpless, pinned, ready for anybody to do God knows what to him.

He wrenched and twisted and pulled and shouted.

"Let me go! Let me go! LET ME GO!"

Suddenly there were people everywhere. People in white. People rushing to him. Let me go! Cut me loose! Set me free!

But they didn't set him free. They held him down. They tightened the bonds. They drove something sharp through his skin and into the flesh of his arm.

2

"Jack?"

He drifted toward the light.

"Jack, come on, wake up!"

Someone was shaking him briskly. Or maybe it wasn't someone. Maybe it was an earthquake.

Jack's eyes popped open, then slammed shut again. Damn, it was bright out there. The light drilled into his brain like a thousand lasers. It wasn't an earthquake after all. It was only Bugs. The unflappable Dr. Bunny.

"What's up, Doc?" Jack said. At least, that was what he meant to say. But his tongue dragged in his mouth, and the words came out muffled, inaudible, incomprehensible. He felt something brush against his lips and opened his eyes again and saw it was a plastic straw. He clamped it between his lips and sucked greedily on it. Then he tried the words again. "What's up, Doc?"

"I thought that was supposed to be my line," Bugs said. He smiled as Jack sucked harder on the straw.

"Yeah," Jack said. His voice was still gravelly, but at least he had control over his tongue again. "But you know me. I'm Daffy, right?" His eyes seared as he shifted them to the right and left, taking in his surroundings. He was in the hospital again. Or still. Maybe he had never left.

Maybe the whole bit about going home had all been a bad dream. Like his recurring nightmare.

"Do you know where you are, Jack?"

No, he wanted to say. I don't know where I am. I don't even know who I am. I don't know anything. Then he could snuggle back into the cocoon — his coma — let it fold right back up over him. And maybe this time he'd be lucky enough never to wake up. Hell, John and Elise Thorne — it was no longer possible to think of them as his mother and father — old John and Elise could have their wish, and what do you know, folks, everyone could be happy.

But he couldn't say that, could he? Because it wasn't true any more. If anything, he knew too much. Or that's how it felt. And he was no longer in a coma. Sure, he could go back to sleep. But eight hours from now, he'd be wide awake.

"Jack? Do you know where you are, Jack?"

His eyes burned as he shifted them back up to Bugs. "Yeah," he said. "I'm in Mercy General, right?"

"Do you remember how you got here?"

Jack tried to move his head. It was too far away, too difficult, his head was too heavy.

"Yeah," he said at last. His throat was sore and dry again. "Yeah, I remember." The words felt strange in his mouth. "I remember."

Bugs's smile seemed to stretch forever, and

the longer Jack looked at it, the longer it got. Jack's eyes felt heavy, too heavy to bear. Slowly they drifted shut and Jack fell, sank, wrapped himself in the bottomless blackness.

3

He was sitting up in bed nine hours later, staring bleakly under the cover of the moulded-plastic tray the nurse had plunked onto his table. Red jello. Cream of something-greyish soup. Cauliflower, maybe. Or mushroom. And a soft-boiled egg. Probably runny and underdone. It occurred to Jack that going home had presented him with at least one welcome advantage — good food.

He dropped the cover back onto the tray and shoved the table away. He was glad that he could do it. In the split-second after he awoke that morning, he'd been terrified that he'd find himself still in restraints. But when he opened his eyes, his wrists were free. And his stomach was rumbling. It was still rumbling.

Jack stared at the tray again. Okay, so it wasn't good food. It was still food. And if he knew Mercy General — and he did, only too well — that tray was all that stood between him and starvation. Or at least between him and the mid-afternoon juice cart. He reached to unlatch the side of his bed, but before he could even locate the latch, the door opened and a tantalizing aroma assaulted his senses.

Bugs grinned from over the top of a large paper bag.

"Hungry?"

Jack nodded. Hungry didn't begin to describe the pain in his belly. It wasn't even in the same country, let alone the same neighbourhood, as the angry ache he felt.

Bugs dropped the bag onto Jack's lap and pulled up a chair. He settled himself into it while Jack ripped open the bag and laid bare a bacon-double-cheeseburger, a large order of fries, a half-dozen packages of ketchup, and a jumbo iced rootbeer.

"Bugs, you're terrific!" he said. He bit deeply into the burger. His stomach almost leaped into his throat to meet the succulent beef.

Bugs watched him in silence for a few bites. "How are you feeling, Jack?" he asked when Jack's appetite eased a little. "What's new?"

Jack leaned back against his pillow. What's new? Trust old Bugs to ask a question like that. "Nothing's new. Nothing's changed. Sorry to disappoint you."

Bugs shrugged nonchalantly. "I don't think I'm the one who's disappointed."

Jack dragged a french fry through a puddle of ketchup. The nothing that had changed included Bugs. He still talked like a shrink. He still was a shrink.

"I remember how I got here the second time," Jack said. "And that's all I remember." He tried to sound like he didn't care, but he did. It was his life they were talking about. His totally screwed-up life. He shoved a french fry into his mouth.

"Some things take time, Jack."

"And some things were never meant to be."

Bugs settled into his shrink pose. He looked benignly at Jack, but said nothing.

Let him look, Jack thought with annoyance. There were times when Bugs drove him right up the wall, which was pretty ironic considering Bugs was supposed to be a mental health expert. Well, let him see how it felt for a while. Let him sweat out the silence.

Bugs waited patiently, like a man with time on his hands waiting for a bus. Jack didn't see a drop of sweat on him. Cool old Bugs. Infuriating old Bugs.

"Damn it, you probably knew about it the whole time, didn't you?" Jack said.

Bugs's eyebrows crept almost imperceptibly up his forehead.

"Don't give me that!" Jack said. "You knew. You've probably been sitting around waiting to see how long it would take me to find out."

Bugs's eyes were as bland as the soup on the tray.

"Jeeze!" Jack said. He crumpled the paper in

which the bacon-double-cheeseburger had been wrapped, stuffed it into the empty fries carton, and pitched it in the trash. "My old man was ready to have them pull the plug on me, and you probably knew all along."

"Actually," Bugs said in an even voice, "I only knew about it after you woke up, after I was called in on a consult."

"But you didn't tell me!"

Bugs's smile was unapologetic. "I'm a doctor, Jack. I treat the most serious problems first."

"Which doesn't include a couple of parents who decide to do their kid in, right?"

Infuriatingly, Bugs said nothing.

"What was it? Was I running up too high a medical bill? Was I taking up a bed needed by someone else? Were they getting too damn tired of coming here to visit me?" A chill ran through him. "Did they even come to visit me while I was here?"

Bugs let the silence ride for a while. Then he said, "What do you think?"

Jack knew what Bugs was going to say before he said it, but still he exploded.

"How the hell do I know what to think? I don't even know my parents, for pete's sake. I didn't even know John Thorne isn't my real father. Did you know that?"

Bugs remained as impassive as stone.

"Well, I didn't know it. They could be a pair

of psychopaths, for all I know. Maybe they've bumped off dozens of kids. Maybe I don't even belong to them. Jeeze, how do I know why they did it?"

"But you care."

It was a statement, not a question. Jack glowered at him. Damn it, he hated it when Bugs was right, when it turned out Bugs could read Jack better than Jack could read a comic book.

"Do I have to go back there?" Jack asked.

"You'll be eighteen in six months," Bugs said. "In the meantime, I think it would be possible for Children's Services to work something out. So, no, you don't have to go back there unless you want to."

"I don't want to."

"I guess that makes sense . . . unless you want an answer to your question, that is. Unless you'd rather not go through life with that question always in the back of your mind."

If Jack had had something handy, he would have thrown it at Bugs.

"I thought you guys were just supposed to sit there and nod every once in a while. I didn't know you also delivered sermons."

"It's not a sermon. It's information, followed by observations. What you do with that information is entirely up to you."

Jack digested this. He studied Bugs's face

but couldn't read it, couldn't tell if he was serious.

"They'll make me go back," he said at last.

Bugs shook his head. "They won't. Your mother was here, Jack. She was very upset . . . "

She was upset? Boy, could he give her a lesson in upset.

" . . . She said she wants you to decide. She'll understand if you don't want to go back home."

She'd probably do more than understand. She'd probably dance with happiness. She wanted to be rid of him — if he didn't go back home, her wish would come true.

"I hate school," he said abruptly. It was another reason not to go back. "I'm not even good at it."

Up crept Bugs's eyebrows again. "You aren't?"

"Okay, so I wasn't. I wasn't good at it."

Bugs's smile was enigmatic. "Maybe you just weren't trying."

"Right. Maybe I'm really the next Albert Einstein."

"I don't think I'd go that far. But your mother told me you did really well in primary school."

Jack rolled his eyes. "In primary school. I peaked in primary school, and it's been a downhill slide ever since. Great."

Bugs was unperturbed. "You have to look at the facts, Jack, before you start drawing conclusions from them."

"Yeah, and the fact is that I'm barely scraping by in all of my classes."

"The fact is that you were barely scraping by. Maybe you were just one of those guys who got distracted by puberty. It happens all the time. A guy grows hair under his arms, and suddenly he goes crazy. It takes maybe a couple of years for him to settle down again."

"And maybe I'm just plain stupid."

Bugs considered the possibility. "There's one way you can find out for sure," he said at last. And then he waited. Jack considered trying to wait him out, trying to make him say what was on his mind straight out, without Jack always having to ask. But what was the point? It would just draw the whole thing out longer than necessary. Because Bugs was the champion waiter-outer.

"How can I find out for sure?" Jack asked. He knew he sounded snotty, and didn't care. He was getting sick of Bugs's psychiatrist shtick.

"You can try, Jack. You can try to do well in school, and see what happens. If you do your level best and still can't manage to pass history and English, then you'll know you can't do it. But you have to try first, Jack. You have to do the experiment before you can draw conclusions from it."

"And I suppose you think I should go back to my parents, right?"

"What do you think?"

Jack sat up straight in bed, and shook his

head angrily. "I asked you first! You're supposed to have the answers. You're the doctor. Just for once, I want to know what you think first."

Bugs regarded him blandly for a few moments. Jack wished he could rip off the shrink's mask that Bugs so often wore. He wished he could see what the real Bugs was thinking.

"I think you have to make a life for yourself. Whether you remember anything from before or not, you still have to make a life for yourself. I think maybe home is a good place to start."

Jack stared sullenly at him.

"She's your mother, Jack, whatever else she is. They are your parents."

They're my parents, all right, Jack thought, and they love me so much they tried to kill me.

"Well, I better get moving along," Bugs said. He slapped his hands onto his knees and pushed himself up from his chair. "I'll drop in on you later."

After he left, Jack sank back against his pillow. It was always such a pleasure seeing Bugs, kind of like having dental surgery. When you had made it through a session, a great light washed over you and you were filled with immense relief that you were no longer sitting in the dentist's chair.

The headache he had awakened with had returned, another side benefit of a visit with Bugs. It was always such a pleasure to dwell on difficult issues. Like whether to go back home.

Whether to face the two people who had gone to court to have his feeding stopped — the two people who had wanted him dead — his step-father and his mother. His mother, for pete's sake.

His mother.

Jack squeezed his eyes shut to block out the picture. Jeeze, why did he have to wake up in the body of such a loser? What was the point of trying to fit back in when what you were trying to fit back into was the life of some poor schmooze whose parents didn't care if he ever drew another breath, whose girl had dumped him the minute he was down, and whose friends and acquaintances seemed more astonished than pleased to see him among the living again?

If he were out on a mountain peak in the middle of nowhere, he would have thrown back his head and yowled with the pain. But he was in the middle of a city hospital filled to overflowing with the sick and the injured, so instead he buried his head in his pillow. Soon it was soaked with tears.

4

The sound was so faint that at first he thought he had imagined it. He opened his eyes and listened.

Someone was knocking at the door. Which meant that it wasn't a nurse. His mother, maybe?

"Come in." He wasn't sure he even wanted to face her. But he was sure he wasn't ready to. His heart leapt into his throat as the door swung open slowly.

It was Cleo Taradash. Her long black hair hung like a cape over her shoulders and halfway down her back.

"Hi, Jack," she said. She gazed around the room with large dark eyes, then peered with concern at him. "I heard you were here. Are you okay?"

He saw her mouth open. He heard her words. But the fact that it was a question that he was expected to answer still managed to take him by surprise. He was too busy grappling with the fact that there was a girl in his room, and that he was lying on his bed in his pyjamas, no robe. He yanked a sheet up over his legs. His cheeks blazed with embarrassment as he wondered how much she had heard, and how much of it was accurate.

"Are you okay?" she asked again, forming her words carefully, speaking slowly, as if she suspected brain damage. "I brought you some homework."

"Homework?" He was sure he had heard her incorrectly. "Did you say homework?"

"Yeah. I — I thought maybe you wouldn't want to fall behind."

For someone who claimed to be making straight As, she suddenly didn't seem so smart. Either that, or she had a wicked sense of humour. "Even if I scored a hundred percent from here on in to the end of the year, I'd still flunk," he said.

She shrugged. "If you scored a hundred percent from here on in, and you went to summer school and earned a hundred percent there, you might be able to make up all of the time you lost. Maybe you could start your senior year in the fall. You could graduate a year behind schedule instead of two."

Bugs must have snagged her out in the hall. Maybe he'd given her some pointers. Talk about school. Tell him you think he can do it. Tell him he's not stupid.

"Sure," Jack said. "And maybe they'll give me the Nobel Prize for chemistry, too."

"Ha, ha," Cleo said drily. She put his books onto his bedside table and dropped lightly into the chair beside his bed. "Seriously, Jack, are you okay?"

He turned away from her and looked out the window. "Sure, I'm fine." As fine as a near-murder victim could feel.

"I heard what happened," she said slowly. "I thought, you know, if it had been me . . . I mean — "

He turned back to her. "What did you hear?" he demanded.

She jumped in her chair. Her cheeks reddened. "I heard what that creep Gary said, and that you didn't know about it before. I thought —"

"You thought?" Suddenly he wished that she'd clear out. "What does this have to do with you?"

She stood up. Good, he thought. Good first step. Now leave.

"I didn't do anything," she said. "I wasn't even living here when it happened. I-I went to the library. I read about it in the newspapers they have on microfiche."

"The newspaper?" God, it just kept getting worse. And worse. "This was in the paper?"

She nodded. "When your parents went to court, it made the news."

His head swam. He felt nauseous. This couldn't be happening to him.

"You mean, everyone knows about it?"

She nodded slowly, almost apologetically. "Everyone who reads the paper, I guess. I'm sorry, Jack."

She was sorry? Jeeze, Jack felt like diving out the window. With any luck, he'd break his neck and it would be all over and everyone would be happy.

"Jack, I'm sure that if your parents had known, they wouldn't have — "

He cut her off. "Do you know my parents?"

"No, but — "

"Then how do you know what they were thinking? How do you know what they wanted?"

The blush on her cheeks turned to a crimson stain of anger. "Well, I don't know, but —"

"But nothing." Jack said. "Jeeze, what am I going to do now?" He stared bleakly out the window. A few minutes slipped by.

"Jack?" Her voice was soft like a wisp of cloud or a bit of cotton wool. He turned slowly to face her.

"I'm tired now," he said dully.

"Don't quit, Jack."

"Cleo, if you don't mind . . . "

Her dark eyes blazed. She planted her hands on her hips. "I mind," she said. "I mind a lot. Look, Jack, I'm sorry about everything that happened to you. And I know you must be feeling pretty terrible right now. But you're still here, Jack, and you still have to live in this world. You just have to face up to it, that's all."

Jack glowered at her. "You sound exactly like my shrink," he said angrily.

She met his furious eyes with a calm gaze. "If you mean that as an insult, forget it," she said. "Some of my best friends are psychiatrists. Well, one, anyway."

"Don't tell me," Jack said sourly. "Your old man is a shrink."

Cleo stiffened but didn't back down. "My old man died a while ago."

He should have said he was sorry. He should have expressed some sympathy. Instead he said, "And I suppose if it hadn't been for your friendly neighbourhood head-shrinker, you never would have made it through, is that it?"

The smile had long since faded from her lips. "Something like that," she said. She picked up her purse and slung its strap over her shoulder. Finally, Jack thought, she's going to leave.

But she didn't leave. Instead she fumbled with the catch on her purse. "I brought you something else," she said. "I don't know why I bothered."

As she rummaged through her purse, he watched her, and wondered himself. She was so pretty. So self-assured. So in charge of her own life. Why was she wasting her time with a loser who couldn't even remember his own shoe size?

"So why *did* you bother?"

She had been burrowing with two hands into a handbag the size of a mailbag, but looked up now, her eyes flashing with anger. "Because I'm an idiot, I guess." Then she sighed. "And because I like you, Jack."

He stared at her in astonishment. There was no hint of sarcasm in her voice. She smiled at him, and his anger dissipated. He suddenly wished he wasn't lying in a sick bed. In his pyjamas. If he could just get her out of his room for a minute so he could slip into his jeans — if he could find his jeans.

"I . . . you . . . you're not bad yourself," he said slowly. How were you supposed to say things like that? And why was it so hard to do? Was it hard for everyone, or just for him?

"Well, thanks," she said, grinning. "A-ha! Found it!" She drew out a sheaf of papers. "Newspaper clippings," she explained. "I made some copies. It's amazing, you know, how they can do that from the microfiche. They come out almost as good as if you photocopied them from a real newspaper."

"Photocopies of what?" Jack said.

"Of newspaper articles."

"About me?"

Her smile faded. "No. But if you want me to . . . "

He glanced at the first sheet.

"They're about that guy Ed Lyle," she said. "I thought, you know, since the guy was your best friend, I thought you'd like to know what happened."

"Thanks."

Her face lit up when she smiled, and he became more acutely aware of the flimsy cotton pyjamas he was wearing.

He scanned the first brief article, then

turned the page. When he looked at the second sheet, he froze.

"Jack?" Her voice seemed a lifetime and a light-year away. "Jack, are you okay?"

Staring up at him was the face from his nightmare. The shattered bloody face, only here it was intact, minus the blood. The face of Ed Lyle.

FIVE

Learn what you are and be such.
Pindar
Odes

1

He pulled on his jacket, zipped it listlessly, then unzipped it again. He closed one hand over the handle of the small overnight bag into which he had packed the toothbrush, comb, and change of clothes his mother had brought from home and left for him at the nurses' station. She had conveyed to him through Bugs that the decision to see her or not lay entirely with him. He had put her to the test. In the three days he was at Mercy General, he hadn't asked to see her once, and she had not appeared. Nor had his father.

Jack reached for the doorknob and hesitated once he held it in his grip. There was still time for him to change his mind. But he'd have to do it now, before he stepped into the hallway, before he left the institutional security of his room.

He didn't have to go out there. Bugs had made it plain enough, had even made a few enquiries on his behalf. There were arrangements that could be made to carry him through the next few months. After that, well, he would be eighteen. His life would be his own. No matter what he did today.

He didn't have to be with the people who had filled his life before the accident — if it was an accident. He didn't have to be in the familiar surroundings that Bugs had told him were his best chance to help him remember. He could turn away from the whole lot of them, just forget they had ever existed — no, better make that not remember that they had ever existed. He could just plunge ahead as if today was the first day of the rest of his life.

The only thing that stopped him from doing that was the fact that it wasn't the first day. That had come two weeks ago. And in those two weeks, he had learned a lot. They had started something for him, and he couldn't walk away until he had finished it.

He twisted the knob and pulled the door open.

His mother was sitting in the small alcove waiting room midway down the hall. She was twisting a white lace hankie in her hands, and he knew the moment he looked into her reddened eyes that she had been crying. Again.

"Jack," she said when he saw him. She started toward him, then stopped halfway, as if she had ploughed into an invisible barrier between them. Her smile was tremulous, her voice small and uncertain. "I'm glad you decided to come back home, Jack."

Jack looked evenly at his mother's tear-stained and swollen face and wished he knew what to say. But he could think of nothing.

"Well," she said after an awkward silence, "I guess we'd better go."

He followed her out of the waiting room, into the elevator, and out onto the pavement where she flagged the first taxi in a line of three. Jack politely opened the door for her, and slipped in beside her. His mother gave their address and Jack settled back into the tension of the back seat. They rode in silence, his mother paid the driver in silence, they walked up to the house in silence. She unlocked the front door.

"Well," she said, setting her purse down onto the hall table, "are you hungry, Jack?"

He shook his head as he looked into John Thorne's study, then listened for other sounds in the house, sounds indicating the presence of other people. There were none.

"Where's . . . " Where's Dad? He would rather choke than refer to that man as Dad, or Father.

Her lower lip trembled. "John is out of town for a few days," she said. Tears welled up in her eyes.

"When is he coming back?" Never would be

too soon.

"I don't know. He . . . he might be gone for a while."

Jack expected the tears to break loose at any moment, but they didn't. She held her head high and her shoulders well back, like a determined soldier.

"Is there something wrong . . . you know, between the two of you?"

"No. I'm not sure. I don't know." She managed a feeble smile. "I'm really glad you decided to come back home, Jack."

Jack nodded brusquely. He wished he was as happy as she was about his decision. He wished he was convinced that he had done the right thing.

"I'm going to put my things away," he said after a moment. He slipped past her up the stairs and breathed a sigh of relief when he was finally alone in his room.

2

Jack closed his bedroom door and flattened himself against it as if he expected his mother to pound it with a battering ram. Nothing happened. He relaxed a little and gazed around the room. There had to be something, he thought, not for the first time. There had to be something somewhere in this room that would give him a clue, that would at least begin to explain to him why his old buddy Ed, missing and presumed a runaway, wasn't missing at all but had steady work as a featured performer in Jack's dreams. And why Jack appeared alongside him with a knife in his hand. A blood-streaked knife.

Okay, Jack thought grimly. If I were a rampaging psychopath, where would I hide evidence of my crime? The bookshelf? The bedside table? The desk? The desk! He ran to it and yanked open the bottom drawer, the one crammed full of old test papers and class assignments. Maybe there was something hidden inside, some scrap of paper, some in-the-margin doodle.

He studied the topmost sheaf of papers. Then the second. And the third and the fourth and the fifth. An hour later the entire contents of the drawer were heaped beside him where he sat cross-legged on the floor, and the only thing he had learned was that he was a poor speller and an even more pathetic grammarian.

Okay, so it's not the desk. Where then? Under the bed?

Under the bed he found one gym sock and a warrenful of dust bunnies. Marguerite was obviously handier with a skillet than she was with a vacuum cleaner.

Nor did he find anything in any of the textbooks in his bookshelf, in any of the *Sports Illustrateds* or the *Playboy* magazines. There was nothing anywhere. Not even a mention of Ed.

He drifted over to his computer and idly flipped through all the game disks. There was nothing on them. He had played them all. And then he came to the unmarked disk at the back of the case. The one without a label. The one that wouldn't work on his machine. He pulled it free from its nesting place and flicked the switch on his computer.

3

A split-second after Cleo said, "Be careful with that, Jack. It's acid. It'll burn whatever you drop it on, including your skin," Jack stepped on something — a pencil or a piece of chalk was what it felt like. Whatever it was, it was round and hard and it had the same effect on him as if he had stepped on a roller skate at the bottom of a flight of stairs. The foot that had borne down on the object shot straight out in front of him. His other foot followed along promptly, as if it were tied by an invisible cord to the first. Suddenly Jack found himself staring at the ceiling and wondering just how much the acid burned. Because as he flew up, so did his hands, and so did the beaker he was carrying, and so did the liquid in the beaker. Jack could see a big wave of it ready to slop over the edge, and, he realized with horror, if he didn't straighten up pretty fast and get that hand under control, it was going to end up plunk in the middle of his lap.

He wrenched his arm back smartly, twisting it, almost wrenching it out of its socket, in fact. Like the coyote when he finally goes off the cliff the Roadrunner cartoons, a big spatter of acid hung suddenly free of the beaker. For a second, it looked like it wasn't going to fall. Then, suddenly, just like the coyote, down it plummeted. It did not land in Jack's lap. It landed on a stack of Cleo's things on the lab bench.

Cleo, who had been hunched over her textbook, reviewing the experiment they were about to do, sprang up and jumped backward in one fluid movement. She looked with annoyance at her stack of binders and notebooks, the topmost of which was smoking and sizzling.

"That's my social studies report," she said. Her voice hissed as menacingly as the acid. "It took me two months in the library to write that thing."

"I-I'm sorry," Jack said. "I slipped."

Cleo snatched the report from the top of the heap and plunked it into the aluminium sink.

"Are you ever lucky that I finally got a computer for Christmas. Because if I had to type that thing all over again just because some klutz didn't look where he was going . . . "

Jack had stopped listening after the first

sentence of her outburst. After the tenth word, in fact.

"You have a computer?"

She looked at him archly, as if he had just lost possession of what few brains she credited him with at that moment.

"Yes," she said tartly. "I have a computer."

"So you know about computers?"

Her indignation faded. A tiny wrinkle, like the faintest crack in a sidewalk, appeared in her forehead.

"I know a few things," she said. "Jack, are you okay?"

"Yeah, sure."

"Because you look kind of funny, you know. You look like you should be standing under a light bulb. One that just went on."

"It's nothing," he said. Well, probably it was nothing. He didn't want to say anything at all until he was sure. He suspected it was inevitable he would come out of this looking a little ridiculous, but he didn't want to make a complete fool of himself.

"But you want to know something about computers, right?" she said. The ease with which she seemed able to read him was unnerving.

"Well . . . yes."

"Shoot."

He stared mutely at her. She was watching him with intent concern now. In a few seconds, she might well be rolling on the floor, helpless with laughter brought on by what she might think was The World's Stupidest Question.

"Come on, Jack, what do you want to know?"

"It's . . . it's nothing."

Coward, he told himself bitterly.

Cleo was right beside him now. Her fresh fragrance engulfed him. "Do you have a computer, Jack?"

He nodded.

"Do you want me to show you how to use it?" She spoke so gently that he shifted his focus from the marble top of the chemistry lab bench, up into Cleo's warm chocolate eyes. She smiled encouragingly at him. "What kind of system do you have?"

What kind of system? He shrugged idiotically. He didn't even know what kind of system he had, for pete's sake.

"I know a little about it already," he said. "I have a bunch of games . . . "

Her interest flagged. "It's not Nintendo, is it?"

Jack struggled to form a picture of his computer in his mind. "No, I don't think so. Anyway, I have this one disk — "

"Oh, then it's not Nintendo," she said. "Nintendo has cartridges, not disks."

"Oh," he said, although he wasn't sure he understood the significance. "Anyway there's this one disk, I can't get it to work."

"What do you mean, can't get it to work?"

"I can't get it to come up on the screen. It just doesn't work."

She thought about that for a moment. "Maybe it's damaged. Or maybe you're just doing something wrong. Look, if you bring it in, I'll try it on my machine at home. You know, see if there's anything wrong with it."

He reached for his own stack of books and pulled something from the back of his three-ring binder. He handed it to her.

She took it and looked at it, then looked evenly at him. "Why do I feel like I'm being taken for granted, and I hardly even know you yet?"

"You're so smart," he said. "I thought there was a good chance if anyone would know, you would."

She grinned at him. "I warn you, Jack, flattery will get you everywhere with me. I'll check it out tonight." She tucked it into the back of one of her textbooks.

"If you don't mind," Jack said, "could you do it after school? And I'd kind of like to be there when you do."

She arched an eyebrow. "What's the matter, don't you trust me?"

"It's not that," he said quickly.

"Well, what then?"

Jack's cheeks began to burn. "It's just . . .

well, I have no idea what's on that disk."

Her chocolate eyes narrowed. "You think it might be something important?"

Jack felt as if he was suddenly engulfed in flame. "I think it could be something embarrassing," he said. "I . . . I want to know, but I'd kind of like to be there, you know?"

She grinned at him. "I don't know where you got the reputation of being some kind of trouble. I think you're kind of cute."

He wouldn't have believed it possible a few seconds ago, but the flames rose higher.

"We can go to my place right after school," she said.

4

After school, Jack walked with her to the bus stop. They rode north for twenty minutes to the other side of the highway where, instead of single family houses on rectangular squares of grass, the buildings were all highrises. Like giant leafless trees they rose from barren beds of cement. The only shade around was the sun-bent shadows of neighbouring buildings. The whole area, Jack thought, would bake like upright loaves of bread in the summer sun.

They had been carried past three dozen buildings when Cleo nudged him and said, "Next stop." She stood and pulled the cord to signal the driver. Jack followed her to the rear door, and held the gate for her when the bus stopped. He jumped down onto the pavement beside her.

She led him into a white brick building that differed from its several dozen neighbours only in the huge number that stood on the breezeway above the front door. She unlocked the inside security door, glanced at the elevators and said, "Let's walk."

Naturally he assumed that her apartment must be on the second floor. Third floor tops. As they climbed toward the fourth, he was panting heavily. Nine months in the hospital had done little to aid his physical stamina. His lungs felt as though they would burst, his stomach churned and threatened to leap out his mouth. He paused midway up to the landing and gasped, "Is it much further?"

"Not much," she called back cheerfully without even looking back at him. "We live on ten."

"Ten?" If he pushed himself, he could make four. He could crawl up to five, maybe six. But ten? "You go on ahead," he said. "I'll wait for the elevator."

She stopped and turned around, talking already, saying, "The elevator? Are you crazy? It's wash day. Every old lady in the building is down in the basement, holding an elevator open until her dry cycle stops. If you wait for an elevator, you could be waiting for twenty minutes."

Twenty minutes of not climbing. The idea washed over him like a cool breeze on a hot day.

"I don't mind," he said.

She looked at him quizzically, then shrugged and said, "Okay, whatever you want." She bounded energetically back down the stairs past him and held open the door to the third-floor corridor. Just as she had warned, they waited twenty minutes after they pushed the up button. Twenty-two minutes, in fact.

"You live here with your mother?" he asked. Standing still had proven a good influence on his ability to speak.

"My grandmother," Cleo said. He expected her to continue, to explain. She didn't.

"Have you lived here long?"

"Since August."

"Where'd you live before that?"

She glanced at him sharply. "What is this, Twenty Questions?"

Well, excuse me, he felt like saying. She could be so nice sometimes. And then, without warning, she could change her mood, bam, so you didn't know what hit you.

"I'm just trying to make conversation," he said, trying to keep his voice light, trying to cool her down. "I'd bore you with the details of my life, but I don't remember any of them."

She smiled sheepishly. "I'm sorry. I didn't

mean to snap." She looked away from him, up at the lights above the bank of elevators, praying, Jack thought, for one to come along and rescue her from me. When she looked suddenly back at him, her eyes were glistening with tears.

"My father killed himself," she said.

"What?" The word just popped out. But he saw immediately that it constituted the stupidest, most thoughtless reaction he could have had to her statement. Her head snapped away from him, her long black hair flew out like a cape.

"I . . . I'm sorry, Cleo." He circled around her so that he could look at her, but she turned away. He edged around to the other side of her, and caught her lightly on the chin this time when she tried to avoid him. "I'm sorry. I didn't mean to . . . well, to sound like that. I just . . . you say unexpected things sometimes." It sounded lame, but it was the truth. How would she have reacted, he wondered, if he had just announced that his mother had stuck her head in the oven? "I . . . I'm sorry about your father."

She held her head high and nodded curtly. "I just wanted you to know, that's all. It's why I moved here. It's why I live with my grandmother."

Jack wondered where her mother was, but didn't dare ask.

One of the lights beside the bank of elevators

glowed red, and an elevator slid in. Jack followed Cleo inside and watched as she punched the button marked ten.

"My grandmother is retired," she said. "She used to work in a meat-packing plant. She worked there from right after the Second World War up until about two years ago. Then she retired." She spoke the words fiercely. Jack thought she spoke them with pride.

"That's . . . " What? Interesting? Hardly. If anything, it sounded brain-numbing. Forty-plus years in the same job, a meat-packing job. " . . . pretty impressive," he finished with as much enthusiasm as he could muster.

Cleo's eyes blazed.

"It's not impressive," she said angrily. "It's not impressive at all. It's boring. It's horrible. She spent forty years of her life sitting on the exact same stool on a shortening-packing line. She watches game shows all the time now, and goes out to play bingo with a bunch of friends who spent forty years sitting on the same line as her."

Jack shrugged. "As long as she's having fun," he said affably.

Cleo glanced sharply at him again as the elevator doors slid open on the tenth floor. "Are you making fun of her?" she said.

"No, not at all." He stepped out of the elevator. She didn't follow him, but stood inside, glowering, until the doors started to close and he had to drop his foot smartly between them to keep them open. "Why would I make fun of your grandmother, Cleo? I don't even know her."

Cleo gazed sullenly at him through the half-closed doors. "Her apartment isn't anything like your house."

He looked at her with genuine surprise. "How do you know what my house is like? You've never been there."

"I know where you live. The houses in that neighbourhood are huge. I bet you have a swimming pool."

He had to think a moment. Come to think of it, he did remember seeing something in the backyard, a big rectangle covered with tarp.

"Yeah, so?"

"So, I just don't want you making fun of my grandmother, that's all," she said.

Jack sighed and shook his head. He reached into the elevator, took her by the hand, and pulled her gently out. The elevator doors slid shut.

"I would never make fun of your grandmother," he said. "I don't care where you live, Cleo, if that's what you're thinking. And I don't judge you by whether or not you have a swimming pool in your backyard, any more than you judge me by how many As I've earned on my report cards over the years. Okay?"

She gazed into his eyes for a moment. "Okay," she said softly.

Cleo's grandmother was a round, robust woman in a grey pantsuit drinking tea out of a mug while she leaned forward toward the television set and shouted out the answers to *Jeopardy*. Jack noticed, as he waited for Cleo to get her attention, that she got almost every one right.

"Grandma? Grandma, this is a friend of mine from school. This is Jack Thorne."

The hair on Mrs. Taradash's head was curly and grey. Her face was scored with a thousand lines. But her chocolate eyes were as bright and wide as Cleo's as she thrust out a hand and said in a booming voice, "Well, hello there, Jack. Nice to meet you." As she vigorously shook his hand, Jack smiled into her dark velvet eyes and felt warm inside. It was pleasant to think that some things might never change.

"I'm just helping Jack with some homework, Grandma," Cleo said. "On my computer, okay?"

Mrs. Taradash nodded. "Just keep the door open, honey," she said, and winked at Jack. As Jack followed Cleo down the hallway on the other side of the kitchen, he heard Mrs. Taradash yell out, "What is Gibraltar?"

5

"So far, so good," Cleo said. She glanced up from the computer monitor. "Are you sure you booted your machine properly?" she said. "Look, here's the directory. You must have done something wrong, Jack."

Jack shrugged. "I guess," he said. "But I read the manual. I tried everything. I just kept getting this message on the screen, and then nothing would happen."

"What message?"

What message? Good question. Forget about my long-term memory problems, Doc. Is there anything you can do about this short-term problem I'm having? "Incompatible something-or-other," he said. "Something like that."

"I'll take a look at it for you sometime, if you want," Cleo offered. She looked back at the monitor. "According to this, Jack, there's only one file on this disk. El. El what, Jack? How's your Spanish?" She glanced at him as if she expected an answer, then blushed. "I'm sorry, Jack. I forgot."

"Me, too," Jack said.

She smiled and looked back at the monitor. "Well, whatever it is, it's a long one. See how many bytes it takes up?"

He looked quizzically at her. "Bytes?"

Cleo rolled her eyes. "You don't know a whole lot about this, do you, Jack?"

"To tell you the truth, I don't know anything. Can you find out what's in that file?"

"Sure. No problem." She pressed a button on the computer. "Uh-oh."

"What?"

"It's a locked file."

"Locked? What do you mean, locked?"

"You need a password to get in. See?" She pointed to the bottom of the screen where he read Password: She grinned at him. "And don't tell me, let me guess, you don't remember the password."

But Jack wasn't thinking about the password. He was thinking about the filename. El. Not El-something. But E.L. Initials. Ed Lyle. He had been right. Ed Lyle was in his dreams for a reason. But why?

"Jack? Hey, are you okay?"

"Huh?" He turned reluctantly from the screen.

"Jack, what's the matter? You look really spooked."

"It's nothing," he said. How could he possibly tell her? "Nothing at all."

6

Jack arrived at school early the next day, deposited his books in his locker, and set about scouring the school and its premises for Mitch.

Coach Bradley found Jack first.

"Thorne! Yo, Thorne!" he called from the end of a hallway. "Come here."

Jack hesitated. He didn't want to talk to Bradley. He wanted to find Mitch.

"Thorne, hey!"

Jack sighed and loped toward the coach.

"You were supposed to come down to the gym, Thorne. We were going to get you back into shape." His eyes danced with excitement as he contemplated the idea.

"If it's all the same to you, Mr. Bradley . . . "

"Coach. Call me Coach."

Jack smiled politely. "If it's all the same to you, Coach, I think I'll pass."

"Pass?" Coach looked stricken. "You can't pass, Jack." He threw an arm around Jack's shoulder. "Look, I'm going to level with you, Jack. Our track team this year? It stinks! There's not a kid on the team with potential. But you, Jack. You have potential. Do yourself a favour. Do me a favour. Do the whole school a favour, Jack. Come down to the gym after school and start getting back into shape."

"But I don't remember — "

"You don't have to remember. Come down to the gym. Work out with the team."

Jack promised to think about it. It was the only way the Coach would let him go.

Jack finally found Mitch in the second floor

men's room, puffing on a cigarette while he combed his hair back out of his eyes. Mitch's eyes popped wide open when Jack's reflection appeared next to his in the mirror. Then a grin leaped to his face. He whirled around to face Jack directly.

"Jeeze, am I glad to see you. You had me worried, Jack. I thought maybe you'd freaked out again, permanently. And, hey, I was going to come and see you. That Gary, he can be a real jerk sometimes. He can say some pretty stupid things."

Jack shrugged. "He didn't say anything everyone didn't already know. Everyone except me, that is."

Mitch squeezed his shoulder sympathetically. "I'm sorry, Jack. It must be rough."

But that wasn't what Jack wanted to talk about. He had other things on his mind.

"Tell me about Ed Lyle," he said.

Mitch dropped his cigarette butt onto the tiled bathroom floor and crushed it under the heel of his boot.

"Ed? What's up, Jackie? I already told you about Ed. He took off."

"Are you sure, Mitch?"

Mitch glanced around the room, ducked his head to check under the stall doors for feet. "What do you mean, am I sure? What are you getting at, Jack? What's the matter?"

Jack wished he knew. "It's just this feeling I have."

"Feeling?" Mitch slipped an arm around his shoulder. "What's the matter, Jack? Did you remember something?"

"He wasn't in the yearbook," Jack said. "That's why I didn't make the connection sooner. He was absent the day they took the pictures for the year book. So it wasn't until I saw the newspaper clipping with the picture of Ed that I got it."

"Got what?"

A shiver ran through Jack as he recalled the horror of recognition. Quickly, he told Mitch everything about the dream he had been having. Well, almost everything. He didn't tell him about the knife, or who was holding it. Mitch listened in silence.

"Jeeze, Jack," he said when Jack had finished. "It's only a dream. It could mean a hundred different things."

"Maybe. But I don't think so." He knew he probably sounded crazy. It was a dream, for pete's sake. Just a dream. Maybe. "It's this feeling, Mitch. Something happened to Ed Lyle. I know it. I think that's why I see him that way in my dream, all smashed up. You have to help me, Mitch."

"Help you?" Mitch pulled back a little from him. "Help you what?"

"Help me find Ed Lyle. Help me find out what happened to him."

He realized only in the silence that followed that he had seized Mitch by the lapels of his jacket and was clinging to them like a drowning man clinging to a piece of flotsam. "You have to help me, Mitch," he said again. What he thought was: you have to help me find out what I did to Ed.

7

Cleo whistled softly when he pushed open the front door. "Nice place," she said as she stepped onto the checkerboard tile of the foyer. "This is the kind of place I'd like to live in one day."

Jack peeked into the den, but saw no evidence that John Thorne had returned. Good. Jack wasn't eager to see him again. The longer he was gone, the better.

"Hello," he called tentatively. He poked his head into the living room. His mother wasn't there. He called a little louder. "Hel-lo!" Maybe she isn't even home, he thought, and found himself hoping that she wasn't. He didn't want to talk to her. He didn't know what to say to her.

"Hel-lo," a voice called back from the kitchen. But it wasn't her voice. It was Marguerite's. She appeared in the hallway, wiping her hands on a snow-white apron.

"Where's my mother?"

"She's out. She'll be back soon. When she comes back, you tell her the chicken's in the oven. I have to go."

Jack nodded. "Come on," he said to Cleo. "Let's go upstairs."

He led her up to his room.

"Not bad," she said as she stepped in. She swung her backpack down onto the desktop. "This place is three times the size of my bedroom, Jack —" She stopped abruptly and Jack saw that she was looking at his dresser. Or, more precisely, at the mirror above his dresser, and at the photo of Leah Bennett — ripped apart and then taped oh-so-carefully back together — that was tucked into the corner of it. She looked away sharply, and when she spoke again, her voice was distinctly cooler. "I guess we might as well get to work," she said.

As she sat down in front of his computer, Jack plucked the photograph from his mirror and slipped it into a drawer.

"So," she said, "the first thing is to make sure your system is running okay." She turned the machine on and waited in silence. Then she began pushing keys. "Well, no wonder," she said almost immediately. "You couldn't read the disk, Jack, because you don't have the software to run it. I thought it might be something like that. Pass me my backpack."

He handed the pack to her. She took it without even looking at him.

"I brought some disks with me," she said. "You know, just in case. What I'm going to do is load the program onto your system. Then you can fiddle away with it to your heart's content."

Jack watched her while she worked at the keyboard, and first inserted disks into, then extracted them from, the disk drive. He didn't have much idea what she was doing, and he didn't really care. He was content enough to be watching the tilt of her head, the piercing concentration she applied to the task, the slender elegance of her long fingers, the firm set of her jaw. He wondered if he had ever been good at asking a girl out, and if so, what were the tricks that he had used, how had he managed to shake off the tremors that were sending his stomach spinning now when he was just looking at her.

"Okay," she said at last, turning in her chair to look at him. "It's all loaded. You want me to show you how it works?" She slid out of the chair before he even had a chance to nod. "Sit down," she said.

He did and she leaned over him. Her perfume engulfed him. Suddenly he didn't care about the disk, didn't care what was on it, didn't care what secrets it contained. He heard barely a word of her instructions.

"I gave some thought to passwords," she said.

"Usually people do one of two things to help them remember their passwords. Either they write them down . . . "

Jack shook his head slowly. "I tore this place apart the other night. There's nothing here. Nothing that I could find, anyway."

"Or," Cleo continued, "they pick a password that has a special meaning to them, something that they could never forget, even if they tried."

Jack looked wryly at her. "I managed to forget my own name," he said, "and I wasn't trying."

That got a smile from her. He basked in its warmth.

"I hate to tell you this, Jack," she said slowly. "But it's even more complicated than that."

Jack frowned. "I don't know what you mean."

"I mean, you could probably remember all you wanted, and you wouldn't be able to crack this one."

Jack was more baffled than ever. "I must be missing something."

She reached for the disk drive and flipped out the disk. "This — " she said, holding it up to him, "it's not yours, Jack."

"Cleo, I don't — "

"You don't even have the software to run it. This disk came from somewhere else, Jack. Someone must have given it to you. Or you must have found it somewhere. But it's not yours." She slipped the disk back into its sleeve and tucked it into the disk holder. "What's this all about, anyway, Jack? What's going on?"

SIX

Better by far you should forget and
* smile*
Than that you should remember and
* be sad.*

Christina Rossetti
"Remember"

1

"I think you should talk to his mother," Cleo said.

Jack set the clean beaker onto the shelf and dried his hands on a piece of paper towel.

"Whose mother?"

"Ed Lyle's mother. I bet you if we talked to her, we could get some kind of clue what the password might be."

"Yeah, maybe," Jack said. He wasn't sure that he wanted another encounter with Mrs. Lyle. The first had been traumatic enough.

"You don't sound very enthusiastic." Cleo tucked her stack of texts and notes under her arm and led the way out of the chemistry lab. "I thought you wanted to find out what's on that disk. I thought you said it was important."

"It could be important," Jack said irritably. "I said it could be important."

"Same thing," Cleo said with a shrug. She appraised him with her chocolate eyes. "What's the matter, Jack? Yesterday you were all fired up about this. You tore your whole room apart again, looking for some clue."

Yesterday, he had been seized by a kind of insanity. He was so sure that the disk contained the key to the puzzle of Ed's disappearance that he could think about nothing else. He knew that the disk had been locked by Ed, and the idea had caught hold of him that maybe he had missed something on his first hunt of the room. Maybe, because he had been looking for the wrong thing then, he had missed the vital clue. So he had started in on his desk drawer again. Cleo had watched him for a while, and then she had joined him in flipping through the pages of all his books and magazines, looking for a notation of some kind.

"I'll go with you if you want," she said now.

"No," he said quickly. Children need someone to go with them. He wasn't a child, and he didn't want her to think of him as one. "No, it's okay."

She nodded firmly, as if he had accepted her offer. "We'll go right after school," she said. "I'll meet you at your locker."

"No," Jack said with alarm. "Look, I don't want to go. I don't see the point."

"Don't see the point?" He saw the spark in her eyes, the one that seemed to ignite her passions. "What do you mean, you don't see the point? Yesterday you told me you were sure this had something to do with Ed Lyle's disappearance."

"The police don't think he disappeared," Jack said. "They think he ran away from home." He was sorry now that he had told her anything. He was even sorry that he had been paired with her in chemistry. "Even his friends think he disappeared."

"Friends? What friends? You were his friend, weren't you? What do you think?"

"It doesn't matter what I think. The cops think he just ran away. So does Mitch."

"Mitch!" Her nose curled in disgust. "I don't get it, Jack. You're such a nice guy. How can you hang around with someone like Mitch Cameron?"

Jack stiffened. "Mitch Cameron was my best friend."

"Was," Cleo said. "I like the way you say that. Past tense. Why don't you just keep it that way?"

Her tone annoyed Jack. "What do you have against Mitch? You're always running him down."

"I don't like him."

"You don't even know him."

Pwoof! Like a match set to dry grass, her eyes ignited.

"You're the one who doesn't know him. I know as much as I ever want to know. I went out with him."

Jack almost fell over from surprise. "You dated Mitch? For how long?"

Her face soured. "About four hours."

Anther surprise. "Four hours? You mean, you had one date with him?"

"Believe me, one was enough. The guy's a total creep. And I don't want you to end up the same way. You don't need to hang around with a creep like that."

A creep like that. What would she think if she knew what kept him up nights, white-knuckled in the blackness of his room? Hey, Cleo, I've got a secret for you. You may think Mitch is a creep, but how about what I am? Can you guess, Cleo? I'll give you a hint. It's something that's never past tense. It's something you can't shake, a tag you wear for the rest of your life. You can never say, "I *was* a murderer." Once you've done it, that's what, forever, you are.

"I don't want to go to Ed Lyle's house," he said, "and I don't want to talk to Mrs. Lyle." He turned abruptly away from her.

"Fine," she yelled after him. "Don't. I'll do it myself."

He wheeled around and glowered at her.

"This is none of your business. It has nothing to do with you."

She met his hostility with calm and determination. "I think you're right, Jack. I think that disk has something to do with your friend Ed. So I'm going to go over to his place this afternoon and I'm going to talk to his mother and I'm going to try to figure out the password that will unlock that file. If you don't want to come with me, that's fine."

And then she turned and walked away from him.

2

Jack stared at the heavy brass knocker in the middle of the dark oak door. He knew he had to grasp it and thump it against the brass plate, but his arm was paralysed. His legs, however, were not. If anything, they had developed brains of their own, and those brains were screaming at him to run in the opposite direction.

"Do you want me to knock?" Cleo asked softly.

"No. No, I'll do it." But still his hand dangled uselessly at his side.

Cleo reached for the knocker. Suddenly Jack's hand came alive. He grabbed her by the wrist and held on.

"I'll do it," he said.

"Then do it."

"I just want to get this clear — how are we going to find out what we want to know?"

"We'll just get her to tell us about Ed. His interests. Maybe he had a favourite sport, a favourite sports figure. Or maybe he has a pet dog."

"What does that have to do with anything?"

"When you make up a password, you have to be sure you won't forget it. If he had a pet, maybe he used its name as the password. Or maybe he used the title of his favourite book, or a character in a favourite book. That's the kind of thing we have to know if we're ever going to crack that file." She reached for the knocker again. "Don't worry, Jack. It's going to be just fine."

This time he let her knock. He also let her speak to Mrs. Lyle. Her calm, soothing voice impressed him, as she explained that they wanted to talk to her about Ed, that Jack wanted to know everything about his old friend Ed, his best friend Ed . . .

" . . . if that's okay with you, Mrs. Lyle. It would help Jack a lot."

Mrs. Lyle hesitated a moment, and searched Jack's eyes. Finally she nodded. There was a catch in her voice when she said, "That would be fine."

She took them into the kitchen. While Mrs. Lyle fussed over pop and packaged cookies, Cleo dropped her bulging handbag onto the table.

"Maybe you should put that on the floor," Jack said.

Cleo shook her head. "The table is fine."

"Oh dear," Mrs. Lyle said, "I only seem to have diet pop."

"Diet is fine." Cleo fiddled in one of the pockets of her bag as she spoke.

"Here you go." Mrs. Lyle brought pop for them and tea for herself. She began to tell them about her missing son.

"He talked about you all the time, Jack." She gazed down into her cup of tea. "You two were inseparable, even when you were little. Wherever Jack went, Eddie wasn't far behind. Philip — Philip was Eddie's father, Jack, I guess you don't remember him — Philip used to call Eddie your shadow, and that's exactly what he was. That's why I was always so sure you'd know something. He always told you everything. Things he would never tell me or his father. He must have told you where he was going, Jack. He must have." Her eyes glistened with tears.

Jack peered into the depths of his diet cola and wished that he hadn't let Cleo talk him into this. He knew more than enough already. And maybe if he asked too many questions, everyone else would find out, too. He wasn't sure he could handle that.

"It's because Jack and Ed . . . Eddie were such good friends that we wanted to talk to you, Mrs.

Lyle. Jack wants to remember. Maybe if you tell us about Eddie, it will help Jack remember." She smiled gently at Mrs. Lyle. "What did Eddie like to do, Mrs. Lyle? What made him happy?"

"Happy?" The question seemed to surprise her. "Well, he loved sports. He loved to watch Jack run. He never missed any of your meets, Jack. That's what they're called, aren't they? Meets?"

Jack nodded, even though he had no idea.

"And he loved baseball. Well, you both loved baseball, didn't you, Jack?" She smiled happily at Cleo as she remembered. "The two of them used to sit in my living room all summer, watching every baseball game they could find."

"Did he have a favourite team?"

"Oh, I don't know." She thought a moment, then a smile sprang to her lips. "He used to talk about the Royals all the time."

"The Royals?" Cleo glanced at Jack as if to ask, what the heck are the Royals? Jack had no idea, and shrugged his reply.

"The Kansas City Royals, dear," Mrs. Lyle said.

"Did he have any favourite players?"

Mrs. Lyle looked puzzled. "I don't know. Is it important?"

"It could be," Cleo said.

"Well, maybe if you named some of the players, I'd recognize them."

Cleo looked helplessly at Jack, who shrugged again. A guy who can't remember his own name is hardly a good candidate for remembering the names of a bunch of people he'd never even met. Mrs. Lyle shifted uncomfortably in her chair.

"Did Eddie have any pets?" Cleo asked.

"Oh, no. He had allergies." She sounded almost apologetic.

"Hobbies?"

Mrs. Lyle smiled again. "He lived for *The Bugle.*"

"The bugle?" Jack said. "He played the bugle?"

"He wrote for *The Bugle,*" Mrs. Lyle said.

"I think she means the school newspaper," added Cleo. "Is that right, Mrs. Lyle?"

Mrs. Lyle nodded. "Eddie always said he wanted to study journalism. He wanted to be like those two reporters on the Washington newspaper. You know, the two who found out about Watergate."

"Woodward and Bernstein," Cleo said.

"That's them. Eddie adored them. I think he's read every word either of them ever wrote. He even subscribed to their newspaper. Eddie always said he wanted to be just like them. He wanted to write a story as important as the ones they wrote."

"And he wrote for the Kennedy High *Bugle*? I'd like to read some of his articles sometime," said Cleo.

"I – I have a scrapbook," Mrs. Lyle said. "I could lend it to you, if you promise to take good care of it."

"We'd like that," Cleo said. "Wouldn't we, Jack?"

Jack nodded on cue.

Mrs. Lyle hurried out of the room, and returned moments later with a large scrapbook. "You will take care of it, won't you?" she said as she handed it to Cleo.

"I promise we will." She handed it to Jack. "How about movies, Mrs. Lyle? Did Eddie have any favourite movies or television programs? Or writers? What did he like to read, Mrs. Lyle?"

Mrs. Lyle's face curled into a frown, but she answered, naming films and books, musicians and writers that Eddie had talked about. She named so many, in fact, that Jack knew he'd be lucky to remember a fraction of them. He wished he had a paper and pencil to jot them all down. He hoped Cleo's memory was better than his own.

"We should have brought a tape recorder with us," he said as he walked down the Lyle's driveway later beside Cleo, Ed Lyle's scrapbook under his arm.

Cleo smiled and delved into her handbag. She held up a small black machine. "I did," she said.

3

Jack flung the baseball digest down in disgust.

"So much for that brilliant idea," he said. "We've covered every team in both leagues. We've run through the entire NBA. We did the AFL. Jeeze, what next, lacrosse?"

Cleo leaned back in her chair and rubbed her eyes. She had been sitting in front of the computer for more than four hours. Her eyes were red from staring at the screen. "You don't have a *Rock and Roll Almanac* in the house, do you?" she asked.

Jack stared at her in astonishment. "You can't be serious. It's after ten. And do you have any idea how many rock and roll artists there must have been over the years?"

Cleo shrugged as if the number were minuscule. "His mother did say he was partial to Motown," she said. "We could start there. Who knows, maybe we'll get lucky."

"Maybe we'll die of old age first. It seems more likely."

"Come on, Jack . . . "

"Come on Jack, what? What are we going to do once we've exhausted rock and rollers? Start in on the *Who's Who* of science fiction? And follow that up with every actor in every action-adventure movie ever made?"

He reached for the scrapbook Mrs. Lyle had

entrusted to them and thumbed through it again. The collection of articles was meagre and hardly the stuff great careers in journalism are made of. Mostly Ed had been confined to reporting the scores of the various Kennedy High sports team. He had written nothing of substance.

Jack smiled wryly. It figured that his best friend would turn out to be just like him — another loser. "How do we know he just didn't pick a password at random, from a dictionary or a thesaurus? Or maybe he didn't pick a word at all. Maybe he picked numbers. Or letters. Hell, he could have used the initials of some obscure character he met at a bus station for all we know."

Apart from an arched eyebrow, Cleo appeared singularly unmoved by his argument.

"He wouldn't have picked something too obscure. If you pick something too obscure, you run the risk of forgetting it."

"So? Maybe Ed wasn't as smart as you. Maybe he did forget."

Cleo stiffened visibly. He had seen that look before. It was body language for, *I'm not going to budge from here and you can't make me.*

"You don't go to the trouble of locking a file unless it's important," she said evenly. "And if it's important, you lock it with a key you don't plan to forget. That makes sense, Jack. It's logical."

He hated it when she was so stubbornly calm.

146

He also hated it when she was right.

"The password could be anything," he went on. "There are too many possibilities. We have to find some way to narrow the possibilities."

Cleo nodded wearily. "That would be nice. How do you suggest we do that?"

"We could talk to someone else who knew him."

"You were his best friend."

"I knew him the longest," Jack agreed. "But remember what his mother said, that first time in school? She talked about Three Musketeers."

Cleo rolled her eyes. "You mean Mitch, don't you? You're going to tell Mitch about this?"

"He might know something."

"Jack, the guy is a jerk."

"He was Ed's friend, too. He might be able to help."

Cleo shook her head in disgust. "Tell me why I find that hard to believe," she said drily.

4

Cleo hesitated at the door to Mario's and glanced at Jack.

"What's this place like inside?" she asked.

"Well, it's . . . it's like a pool hall, I guess." He tried to recall anything about it that leapt out at him. "You know, tables, cue sticks . . . "

"I know what a pool hall looks like," she said. "I just meant . . . never mind. I don't know what I meant." She sounded annoyed.

"You don't have to come inside if you don't want to. You can wait here."

"I don't think you should go inside," she said. "I don't think you should be hanging around with a guy like Mitch. And I don't think this is any of his business."

He couldn't understand why she disliked Mitch so much, but he had a feeling it wasn't fair. "Mitch is my friend — "

"*Was* your friend. And you used to be a real nitwit in chemistry. You're not such a nitwit any more."

He smiled happily at the compliment. "You think so?"

"I think so," she said. "So let's go."

"I have to talk to Mitch. You may not like him, but he was Ed's friend, and he's mine. He's not such a bad guy, Cleo. Maybe you should give him a chance."

"He had a chance," Cleo said. "He blew it." She stared at the grimy glass set into Mario's front door. "Well, if we're going to do it, I guess we'd better do it." She pushed the door open and led the way inside.

Once his eyes adjusted to the gloom of Mario's, it took Jack only a moment to locate Mitch at a table shooting pool with Gary. He looked up from a shot he was scouting and smirked at Cleo.

"I can't stand that guy," Cleo hissed in Jack's ear.

"Do you want to wait outside?"

"No."

Mitch straightened and leaned on his cue. "Hi, Jack," he said. "You're going to need a warmer jacket if you're hanging around with the Ice Queen there."

Jack glanced at Cleo, who stiffened.

"I guess you two know each other," Jack said.

Gary stepped forward and appraised Cleo with keen eyes. "I don't believe I've had the pleasure," he said.

"I don't know what pleasure you're talking about, Gary," Mitch said. "This one always says no. It's getting so that people are starting to talk. You know, does she even — "

"Knock it off," Jack said sharply. He didn't know exactly what had gone on between Cleo and Mitch, but he knew for sure now that something had. He made a mental note to find out what it was. Later. First things first. "I need to talk to you, Mitch," he said, and cast a glance of significance at Gary.

Mitch followed it and shrugged. "Sure," he said. "No sweat, right, Gary?"

Gary responded with the merest suggestion of a shrug.

"Over here," Mitch said, nodding to a table near the dust-streaked window. When Cleo started to follow them, Mitch turned to Jack and said, "Hey, if you want to talk to me, you talk to me."

Jack saw a pair of sparks suddenly gleam in Cleo's eyes.

"No problem." He peered into her eyes when he said the words, and prayed that she was as good at reading him as he had come to be at reading her.

The sparks caught fire. She rolled her eyes in disgust, but she also nodded. "No problem," she muttered. As she stood at the edge of the pool table, watching Mitch and Jack walk away, Gary sidled up to her.

"So," Mitch said as he slid onto a chair and patted his pockets for his pack of cigarettes, "is there something going on between you and Frosty the Snowlady?"

Jack glanced back at the table. Gary was leaning nonchalantly against it, staring at Cleo through lazy, smoky eyes. He was saying something to her. From the mask of disdain that Cleo wore, it wasn't something she wanted to hear.

"She's my lab partner," Jack said. "She's okay."

"If you're wearing a snowsuit and you're prepared for a long winter, sure, she's a blast," Mitch said. He slipped a cigarette between his lips and produced a lighter from his pocket. "What's up, Jack? You want to ask me more questions about Ed?" He grinned at Jack's surprise. "My old lady and Ed's old lady are in touch a lot. My house is two doors up from his. But I guess you don't remember that, Jack, do you?"

"It's about Ed," Jack acknowledged. "I want to know if there was anything he talked about a lot. A song or a ball player or a movie."

Mitch's eyes narrowed behind wisps of cigarette smoke. "What's going on, Jackie? Why are you asking so many questions about Ed?"

"I already told you."

Mitch laughed. "Right. You told me. You told me about some crazy dream you've been having. What's the matter, Jack? You starting to believe your dreams? You starting to think that someone really did old Ed?"

"Did him?"

"Killed him."

The colour drained from Jack's face.

Mitch peered at him. "Hey, I was just kidding, Jack. You don't think that, do you? You don't really think old Ed was . . . bumped. Do you?" He leaned forward across the table. Two jets of smoke streamed from his nostrils. His eyes burned with intensity. "You sure there's nothing about your dream you aren't telling me, Jack? Are you keeping something from me?"

Am I keeping something from you? You bet,

Mitch old pal. I'm keeping it all from you. But I'll give you a hint. They've made movies about this guy's life. Give up, Mitch? Do you? Does the name Jack the Ripper mean anything to you?

"What's the matter, Jack? You want me to help you find out something, but you don't trust me enough to tell me what it's all about, is that it? When you went to sleep nine months ago, you and me were the best of friends. And now that you're awake, hell, suddenly you're a guy who hangs around with cold-blooded bookworms, and you don't trust your old buddy Mitch."

Mitch ground his cigarette butt into a tin ashtray. "Okay, Jackie, if that's the way you want to play it. You were my best friend, you're still my best friend, so sure, I'll tell you anything you want to know. And if you don't want to trust me, well, there's not a hell of a lot I can do about it, is there?" He leaned back in his chair and stared up at the ceiling for a moment. "What do I know about Ed? Well . . . "

"I found a disk," Jack said. Mitch was his friend. Still. And it was true what he said — if you can't trust your friends, who can you trust? "I found a computer disk. I think it belonged to Ed, and I think there's something on it that can maybe tell me what happened to Ed."

"You think? Don't you know?"

"The disk is locked. You need a password to get in."

Understanding flickered in Mitch's eyes. "And you don't know the password. Which is why you're asking all these questions, right?"

Jack nodded and hoped that Mitch was satisfied. It unnerved him to find Mitch peering even more deeply into his eyes.

"What else?" he asked.

Jack struggled to keep a mask of impassivity in place, but nothing he could muster stood up to Mitch's scrutiny. He glanced over at Cleo and saw that she was still occupied in trying to dodge Gary. Then he leaned in close to Mitch and lowered his voice. "I think it's me," he said. His voice was hoarse, his throat suddenly dry.

"You?"

"I see me with a knife." Just saying the words aloud like that conjured up the mist-swirled picture. "I see me with a knife and I see him, all . . . all covered in blood. I don't think he just disappeared, Mitch. I think — "

"You think you had something to do with it?"

A tremor ran up Jack's back. He nodded slowly.

Mitch started to smile, as if it were all a joke. Then, as he studied Jack, his budding smile faded.

"Hey, Jack, it's just a dream. Dreams don't mean anything. Ed took off, that's all. He couldn't stand the heat at home, so he left. Simple."

Jack wished he could believe that. But he

couldn't shake the feeling that it wasn't simple.

"Jeeze, Jack," Mitch said, "you've got to get a grip on yourself. You didn't tell her about this, did you?" He glanced over at Cleo. "People could get the wrong idea."

Jack shook his head. "She knows there's a disk. That's all she knows."

"Good," Mitch said. "Because you know what I think? I think the less you say about this crazy dream, the better for you."

"But I want to know."

Mitch held his lighter to the tip of the cigarette and inhaled deeply. "What for?"

"What for? Well, because — "

"The guy just ran away from home, Jack. The cops looked into it and that's the way they wrote it off. Runaway. You have any idea how many runaways there are in the country every year? Thousands, that's how many. So why don't you just let it lie? Forget the whole thing and concentrate on getting yourself back into shape again. Look after yourself, Jack, and let Ed look after himself."

The thought was tempting. Besides, Mitch was probably right. It was just a dream, that's all. A stupid nightmare.

"Come on, Jack," Mitch said. "What do you say you ditch the girl and you and I play some serious pool? You could use a few pointers on your game, if you ask me."

"Yeah," Jack said. He stood up. "Maybe another time, Mitch, okay?"

5

His mother sat at one end of the dining table in front of an untouched plate of chicken and snow peas. A bottle of red wine, uncorked and two-thirds depleted, stood by her plate. Nearby lay a sheet of paper and a torn envelope. She looked up at Jack with weary eyes when he stuck his head into the room. When she finally spoke, she shaped each slurred word carefully.

"Hello, Jack. I wasn't expecting you. Are you hungry?"

"I ate already," Jack said.

He had grabbed a burger on his way home and was planning to head straight back up to his room to work on cracking the coded disk, despite Mitch's advice. He knew it probably sounded weird. To Mitch, he looked like he was obsessed — by a dream, for pete's sake.

But it was something more than a dream that had seeped dankly into his bones. More than a dream had shrouded him in a heart-stopping, mind-numbing sense of dread and foreboding. The suspicion that he himself was the monster he was afraid of was what really propelled him into action.

His mother looked at him and managed a

wan smile. She lifted the wine glass to her lips and drank deeply from it. "I don't see much of you any more," she said.

She set the glass sloppily onto the edge of the table, where it teetered before falling and shattering on the floor. She grabbed for a napkin, and, in doing so, upset the bottle and sent the paper fluttering to the ground. Wine cascaded off the edge of the table and drenched the cream-coloured skirt she was wearing.

"Damn," she muttered as she stooped to gather the shards of glass. Then she yelped with pain. Jack darted forward.

"Are you okay?"

She held up a hand. At first Jack thought that the redness on it was wine. Then he realized it was blood.

"I'll get a bandage," he said, and started for the upstairs bathroom.

"No, it's okay," she said. "It's just a nick. It's fine."

She wound a linen napkin around her hand and picked up the rest of the pieces while Jack watched for a moment in silence. Then he reached for a second napkin and mopped up splashes of wine. He lifted the sodden sheet of paper and blotted it with the napkin. He couldn't help reading the first few words, then he couldn't stop himself from reading the rest of the short letter from John Thorne.

"He doesn't say when he's coming back," he said.

His mother snatched the sheet from him, tearing it. Her lower lip began to tremble. "He just needs some time," she said. "Everything's going to be all right. I know it is. He just needs some time."

"He says his lawyer will contact you. That doesn't sound good." In fact, it sounded like divorce.

She wiped a tear from the corner of one eye. "I have a headache, Jack," she said. "I think I'll go and lie down, if you don't mind."

In silence, Jack watched her go. Her footsteps as she ran up the stairs were overlaid with the sound of sobbing. He could hear it fading into the upper reaches of the house.

He crept up to his own room and sat in front of his computer for an hour, but his mind kept wandering from the task at hand. He couldn't stop thinking about his mother, alone and crying. Finally he flipped the computer's off switch and headed for her room.

He stood outside the door for a few moments, listening to the silence within. Maybe the last thing she wanted right now was to talk to him. There was only one way to find out.

He tapped lightly on the door. There was no answer. He stared down at the rose-coloured carpet and told himself that he had tried. He had come down the hall to her room and he had knocked. She had probably fallen asleep. And if she had fallen asleep, then she must not be feeling too bad, right?

Wrong. He knew from experience that everyone had to sleep sometime, even people who felt terrible inside. He felt he had to do something. She was his mother, after all. That meant he was supposed to do something to make her feel better. He rapped more loudly this time.

Her voice was thin when she called for him to enter, and his heart sank. She was still upset. As he twisted the doorknob and pushed the door open, he practised the two words over and over in his head. I'm sorry. I'm sorry. I'm sorry.

"I'm sorry, Jack," his mother said. She was sitting on the edge of her bed. Her eyes were no longer red. Her face looked freshly scrubbed. He guessed that she had composed herself with splashes of cold water. "I – I wanted everything to be perfect when you came home. And . . . well, it isn't perfect at all. It's terrible. You have to understand about your father, Jack . . . "

His father. He couldn't think of John Thorne as his father, not after what he had learned about him.

" . . . Your father never wanted to hurt you, Jack. He just thought . . . they told us you might never wake up, Jack. At first I didn't believe them. I sat by your bed all day every day, I was so sure everything was going to turn out all right. I was convinced you were going to wake up and we would be able to bring you home and everything would be just fine."

Her chin quivered. A tear slipped down her cheek. She rubbed it away. "Your father was there, too, Jack. He couldn't be there all the time, the way I was. He had to work. Someone had to work, Jack. And then . . . " Her lips trembled. More tears overspilled her eyes. She rubbed them away. "After two months, I got sick. My doctor said it was stress and exhaustion. And your father had to bring me home and I couldn't be with you all the time and . . . " Tears flowed freely now. ". . . and you didn't get better and I began to believe that maybe you really wouldn't wake up. M-maybe you would just lie there, forever — in pain. Sometimes you looked as though you were in pain."

She blotted her damp face with a tissue. "I couldn't stand to see you suffering like that, Jack. Neither could your father. We talked about it. We decided —" She broke down completely and started to sob. "I'm sorry, Jack. I'm so sorry. If I had known, I never would have agreed. Your father never would have agreed, Jack. He loves you."

Jack pulled up the few pictures he had acquired of John Thorne, but couldn't imagine how the word love might fit into the frames.

"I know he loves you," his mother repeated as she wiped away her tears. "I know it. I just don't know if he's ever going to be able to live with what we almost did. He cried for hours when you finally woke up. 'I almost killed my son.' That's what he said, Jack. Over and over. 'I almost killed my son.'"

She wept wretchedly, while Jack sat beside her on the bed and watched her, searching for even the tatters of a memory of the things that linked them together. But he saw nothing except a woman's tears.

6

Cleo leaned her long slim body against the locker next to his and said, "There's a dance here tomorrow night. Are you planning to ask me?"

Jack stared mutely at her. The idea had never occurred to him. He hadn't even known there was a dance impending.

"Because if you are," she continued, "you'd better ask me soon. I'm not going to keep turning down other guys, and then find out at the last minute that you've asked someone else. Or that you've been planning all along to hang out at the pool hall with your buddy Mitch."

Jack thought about it for a minute. "I haven't made any plans."

"Is that an invitation?" Cleo said.

Jack smiled. "Yeah," he said. "I guess it is."

When Jack told Mitch what he had done, Mitch laughed and shook his head simultaneously. "You're going to the dance with the Snow Queen? I don't know, Jack. Sometimes I think I should just whack you over the head. It always works in the movies. A guy's got amnesia and the next time he gets whacked over the head, it all comes back to him. Maybe if I were to whack you over the head, you'd at least come to your senses. It's a waste of time going anywhere with her."

When Jack told his mother, she became flustered. "But I won't be here tomorrow night, Jack. I-I have my meeting."

She always went out Friday night. She always said she was going to a meeting. But she never said what kind of meeting, and Jack had the feeling that he wasn't supposed to ask.

"It's okay," he said. "You can go to your meeting."

"But I won't be able to see you off."

It took Jack five full minutes to reassure her that he didn't mind, that he would manage. Then, on Friday evening, when it occurred to him that he had no idea how to dress for a dance at Kennedy High, he wished that she had cancelled her dinner and her meeting and was there to give him some advice. As it was, he stood in front of his closet for ten full minutes, examining the shirt on this hanger, the pants on that, the sweater in the second drawer.

In the end, he decided to strive for the median, and dressed casually but not too casually in pants and a shirt, topped with one of his leather jackets. He checked himself in the mirror, back and front, until he was satisfied that he looked neat even if he turned out not to be dressed appropriately.

"You look terrific," Cleo said when she admitted him to her grandmother's apartment. She looked more than terrific in a short red skirt and a clinging black top that fell off her shoulders.

When they finally arrived at Kennedy High and made their way into the gym, he discovered that for once he had guessed right. His outfit blended in perfectly with what everyone else was wearing. Now if he only knew whether or not he could dance.

He quickly discovered that he could. It just sort of came to him. He didn't have to think about it. He found himself slipping into the movements, as though his muscles and nerves were responding to the pulsing music without any intervention from his brain. He also discovered that he liked to dance. Especially the slow ones, when Cleo came into his arms and her perfume and her softness and her warmth filled his senses.

The music ebbed and he parted from her

reluctantly. His hand was still warm from resting on her silky back. She smiled gently into his eyes.

"It's warm in here," she said.

He had thought it was just him. His shirt was damp under his jacket. Perspiration trickled down his forehead.

"How about a cold drink?" he said. He took her hand into his and led her across the dance floor as the music began to pulse again.

A blonde in a sapphire dress stood at one end of the refreshment table. Jack's heart slammed to a stop. No wonder he had fallen for Leah Bennett once upon a time. She was slim and graceful and held her head high with all the poise of a fashion model. She was so beautiful that Jack didn't notice her escort until he stood directly in Jack's path.

"There's a Coke machine out in the hall," Todd said. "If you want a drink, you can get one there."

"Why don't you just save it for the gridiron, Strasser?" Cleo said. She looked decidedly unimpressed by Todd's bulk and the obstacle he posed. "We can get a drink here if we want to."

Todd looked nonplussed. He gaped at her.

"Come on, Jack," Cleo said.

But Jack's eyes had sought out Leah again and, once they found her, she was all he saw. "Hi," he said.

"Hi, Jack." Her voice was soft and gentle as a summer shower. She looked frightened and determined all at the same time. Frightened of what, he wasn't sure. But determined, he knew, not to run from her fear. Determined to face it down.

Cleo tugged lightly on his hand and he knew he should go, but he couldn't turn away from Leah. He heard Cleo's sigh beside him, long and disappointed.

"Why don't you ask her for a dance, Jack?" she said.

"No you don't!" Todd boomed.

Cleo fixed him with a sour look. Then she turned to Jack. "Go ahead," she said. "For old time's sake, if for no other reason. I don't mind sitting this one out."

Jack searched her face for sarcasm, but found only sincerity. "Are you sure?"

"I'm sure."

"Over my dead body," Todd said. He stepped forward to block Jack's path, but Cleo hooked one of his arms and pulled him back.

"Haven't you heard, Todd? Women make up their own minds now. If Leah doesn't want to dance with Jack, all she has to say is no."

Leah didn't say no.

Todd tried to pull free of Cleo, but she held tight.

"Why don't you relax, Strasser? It's only one dance."

As Jack led Leah onto the dance floor, he heard Todd say, "What makes you so sure?"

7

He took one of her small hands in his. For a few seconds, his free hand hovered like a hummingbird a few centimetres from her back. When he finally found the courage to land it, his hand and arm came alive with the electricity of her warmth. She nestled like a sigh against his shoulder for a moment. The scent of her, like wildflowers, stirred something in him.

"Leah," he said. It sounded like a prayer.

She pulled back from him just enough so that she could look into his eyes.

"I came to see you, Jack. Every day for two months I came to see you." She spoke defiantly, as if daring him to challenge her.

"I know," he said.

She pulled back a little more in surprise. "You do?"

"They told me. But they didn't say who you were. Maybe they didn't know." Although the thought haunted him — that his mother had known, but hadn't told him.

"Maybe," she said. She was silent for a few moments, and then her eyes filled with tears. "I came, Jack. I came until my parents said I couldn't any more. They made me stop. And everyone said you were never going to wake up, that you were going to be in a coma forever, until you . . . " Her voice faltered. Tears streamed down her cheeks. Jack pressed her head against his shoulder and held her tightly.

"I know," he whispered in her ear. "I know."

"And then I met Todd." She wept into his jacket. "I'm sorry, Jack. I'm so sorry."

He held her and calmed her. "Is he good to you, Leah?"

She looked at him and he knew the answer without having to hear it from her lips. Leah nodded.

And what about me? he wanted to ask. Wasn't I good to you?

"Don't cry, Leah. It's okay. Everything's going to be okay, Leah."

When the music ended, he smiled at her and rubbed a smudge of mascara from her cheek with his thumb.

"I must look like a mess," she said.

"You look beautiful." It was the truth. "Come on, we'd better get back to our dates."

A smile lit up her face. She leaned forward and kissed him lightly on the cheek.

"Thanks, Jack," she said.

"For what?"

"I don't know. For being you."

Todd claimed Leah before they were even off the dance floor, and led her away.

Jack joined Cleo, who was sipping a Coke. She offered him an ice-cold bottle, which he accepted cheerfully.

"So," she said while she watched him. "How was it?"

"Okay."

"Okay?" She arched an eyebrow. "Just okay?"

He smiled at her. "Thanks."

"For what?"

"I don't know. For being you, I guess." He was aware of the echo of Leah, even as he kissed Cleo on the lips lightly. She tasted cool and sweet.

"Well," she said, "just so you don't get any ideas, that was a one-time only deal. For the rest of the night, you're mine."

"No problem," he said with a grin. He glanced around the gym.

"Looking for your next partner?" she asked drily.

"Looking for Mitch. I thought he might be here. But I don't see him."

"I can't tell you how sorry I am to hear that," Cleo said. "Come on. Let's dance."

8

Jack knew something was wrong from the moment he shrugged around the corner and saw a police cruiser and an unmarked Chevy sitting in the driveway. Both of them had cherries on top, and both of the cherries were spinning, shooting off beams of red light in all directions. He broke into a run.

A uniformed cop looked up from his notebook when Jack burst into the house. A plain-clothes officer talking on the hall phone glanced at him, and Jack saw it was Lieutenant Mahoney. Mahoney held up a hand, like a traffic cop bringing the east-west flow to a halt. He said a few more words into the mouthpiece, then hung up.

"You been out all night?" he said.

Jack nodded distractedly. His mother wasn't in the living room, and there was no light on in the study. He peered down the hallway that led to the kitchen and saw that there were no lights on back there, either.

"Your mother is fine," said Mahoney.

"Where is she?"

"Upstairs. Lying down. The maid is with her. Marguerite."

Jack relaxed a little. She was probably better off with Marguerite than she would be with him. Marguerite would know what to say to her, how to comfort her. So far he hadn't done a very good job of that.

"What happened?" he asked Mahoney.

Mahoney crouched a little as he looked at Jack, as if he was trying to get a good look into a darkened building. "You really don't remember me, do you, Jack?"

"Yes I do," Jack said. "You came to see me when I got back from the hospital. My mother said you pulled me from the car."

Mahoney laughed. "I mean from before. You don't remember me from before. I can actually see it in your eyes."

Before. The word made Jack's stomach flip. These were the moments he dreaded. The times when he realized most people knew more about him than he did, and they were going to tell him what they remembered. But he never knew what was coming, whether it was good or bad, or even whether he wanted that particular memory back.

Mahoney looked at the uniformed officer. "See what you can get on that make and colour of car," he said.

As the officer left, Mahoney turned back to Jack, probed a little deeper with his eyes, then shrugged. "Life can be funny sometimes, right, Jack? It used to be I could look at you and see a kid headed for big trouble, dragging through school the way you did, ducking off classes. But now . . . " He shrugged. "Now I'm not so sure, Jack. You look like a different person."

Jack stared at Mahoney a moment, trying to ignore the knot in his stomach. Then he started up the stairs. Mahoney caught him by the elbow. "I want to ask you a few questions, Jack."

He knows, Jack thought. He knows something about me . . . and Ed. He turned with apprehension.

"Your mother came back from her support group tonight — "

"Support group?"

Mahoney looked surprised. "Yeah. She goes to a group once a week, to talk about what happened."

Jack wasn't sure he understood.

"It was in all the papers, Jack. Everyone who knew your parents, and a whole lot of people who didn't, read about how they went to court to fight for your right to die. . . . "

Right to die?

" . . . That's a lot of guilt to live with, Jack. So she goes to this group once a week. And when she came back tonight, she found the place had been tossed."

"Tossed?"

"Burglarized," Mahoney said. "And vandalized."

Jack spun around to the living room. Everything looked in order there. He saw no signs of wanton destruction. In fact, it looked as though nothing had been touched. He looked for some explanation from Mahoney.

"That's a funny thing, Jack. The downstairs is as neat as a pin. All the action was upstairs. In the bedrooms."

"The bedrooms?"

"Your mother's room, mostly. Her jewellery is missing. Near as we can tell, nothing is missing from your room. But the place was trashed. Completely ripped apart." He paused a beat. "Your mother tells me that your father's out of town."

"What?"

"I hear your folks haven't been getting along too well, Jack. Do you think your father could have done this?"

"My father?" Jack blinked in confusion. "Why would my father —"

"Come here," Mahoney said, heading through the living room, and into the dining room. "See there?" He gestured toward the sliding door that led out onto a terrace. "That's where the burglar came in."

Jack stared at the door. It was open a crack and smudged along its edge with some kind of powder.

"We dusted for prints, but we didn't find any," Mahoney said. "We figure whoever-it-was was wearing gloves."

Jack nodded. As the silence between them stretched, he wondered if Mahoney were waiting for him to draw some logical conclusion.

"The thing is," Mahoney said, "whoever-it-was who broke in here, he — for the sake of argument, let's say it was a he — he came in through this door, which means he passed through the dining room, which means he saw that it was loaded with silver and gold. He went on up to the second floor where he stole your mother's jewellery, then he went to a lot of trouble trashing your room — and I mean a lot of trouble, Jack, you're going to have to redecorate. He took all that time up there to make your room look like a garbage dump , then he waltzed back downstairs, right past this little Fort Knox your mother has here and out the door — "

"Maybe my mother surprised him when she came home."

"That's not the way it looks, Jack. I've been in this business a long time, and if there's one thing I know, it's when something doesn't feel right. This doesn't feel right, Jack. This doesn't feel like a regular burglary."

The lights came up slowly but gradually, the way they did in a theatre after the last curtain call.

"So you think John . . . my, uh, father had something to do with this?"

"When marriages break up, all kinds of nasty things happen. And it's no secret the way you and your old man got along."

Maybe it was no secret to the rest of the world, but it was one big question mark for Jack. Mahoney seemed to realize that. He shook his head slowly.

"Let's just say you and your dad didn't get along and leave it at that. It would sure explain why someone would take your room apart when, according to your mother, there was nothing missing from it."

Jack felt numb all over as he nodded. That would explain it, he agreed. He felt suddenly drawn to his mother's room.

"Is she in any danger?"

"I don't know," Mahoney said. "With burglaries, if you pay attention, you can see the patterns, you can make some predictions. With divorces . . . " He shrugged. "Well, no two are alike. Your old man has a hot temper, Jack. So we're going to check out where he was tonight, and what he was doing. Okay?" He squeezed Jack's shoulder.

Jack nodded. "Thank you," he said.

Mahoney looked startled, then a slow smile spread across his face. "I used to be so sure about you, kid," he said. "Now . . . I think you could go either way. I think you've got a chance."

Sure, Jack thought as he watched the detectives and the uniformed officers leave. But what would Mahoney think if he knew what Jack suspected?

Jack locked the front door, secured the sliding door of the terrace, then switched off all the lights, and headed upstairs. As he climbed, he caught the scent of perfume. The closer he got to the top of the stairs, the more overpowering the fragrance became. Or, rather, the fragrances, for it seemed to Jack that what he was inhaling was a cacophony of aromas, not a single scent.

When he got to his mother's room, the scent was almost suffocating, despite the windows opened wide on either side of her bed. His mother was sitting up, on top of the covers, one slim hand extended to Marguerite, who was applying red polish to her nails. Elise Thorne's eyes were almost as red as the polish. It was clear she had been crying. Both seemed oblivious to the eye-stinging perfume cloud in whose midst they were seated.

"Jack!" his mother exclaimed. "Jack, I'm so glad you're here!"

"Are you all right?" Jack asked.

"She's fine," Marguerite assured him. "Aren't you fine, Missus?" She applied the last bit of polish to the nail of his mother's little finger, and swirled the top of the bottle into place. "There you are. There's nothing like a good manicure to make a woman feel better." She heaved her body out of the chair. "Well, I can go now, I can see that. The man of the house is here to look after you." She smiled generously at Jack on her way out.

Jack surveyed the room. It didn't look nearly as ransacked as Detective Mahoney had led him to believe.

"Marguerite was an angel," Jack's mother

said. "She came as soon as I called her. And she tidied up my room for me. You should have seen it, Jack. Everything was on the floor. All my perfume bottles were smashed. Every single one of them."

"Do you think my . . . Lieutenant Mahoney said he thought maybe my . . . father . . . " He couldn't believe how difficult it was to say the word. "That he had something to do with this."

She looked appalled. "He wouldn't do something like this," she said. "Not John. He's not like that."

"The police are going to find out."

"But he wouldn't," she said. "He's scared about what happened. He feels so guilty. But he would never do this, Jack. You have to believe that."

When he couldn't tell her that he did, she started to cry. "Oh, Jack," she said, "you should see what they did to your room."

They — he — had, quite simply, reduced everything in the room to rags and rubble. The clothes had been torn from his drawers and shredded. The books and magazines had been pulled from his shelves and destroyed. His mattress had been slashed. Videotapes, audiotapes, computer disks, all lay smashed and mangled on the debris-littered floor.

As Jack walked toward his desk, something crunched underfoot. He stooped to retrieve a mangled computer disk. Ed Lyle's disk. Tears of rage streamed down Jack's cheeks.

Everything, absolutely everything was ruined. That bastard John Thorne had demolished the only chance Jack had to decode the nightmare that had plagued him for as long as he could remember.

SEVEN

Between friends there is no need of justice.

Aristotle
Nicomachean Ethics

1

Jack scrambled for the door at the first chime of the bell. It was Marguerite's day off, and his mother was upstairs napping. She had barely slept the night before and had appeared at breakfast with dark circles under her eyes. Now, after spending the whole day straightening up first her room, then, with him, his own, she was asleep. He didn't want her disturbed. He swung the door open and stared at the figure on the porch

"Cleo." She had called him half an hour before to see if he wanted to go to a movie, and he had told her briefly about the break-in. She had sympathized, but said nothing about dropping by.

"Jack, are you okay?" She managed a smile, but it did nothing to hide her concern.

"I'm fine." It was nice to know that she cared.

"I can't say the same for my room, though."

"It must be awful." She shuddered. "I can just imagine how I'd feel if someone broke into my place and wrecked everything I own. And you have better stuff than me. You must feel terrible, Jack."

Jack shrugged. "I don't mind so much about my stuff," he said. "It's not like it has sentimental value. With my mother's stuff, it's different. She feels pretty bad."

"Is she okay?"

"She's sleeping."

"Do the police have any idea who did it?"

"Not really." He peered into her chocolate eyes. Now that the disk is ruined, he thought, whatever was on it is gone for good. And maybe that was for the best. Because Mitch was probably right — Ed had just taken off. Thousands of kids took off every year. Ed was just one more. And Jack's dream was just that, a dream, a bunch of crazy mixed-up images of people he used to know once upon a time. That was then, and this was now. And Cleo was now, too.

"I-I was just going to get myself a cold drink," he said. "You want one?"

He poured cola over ice in the kitchen and offered her Marguerite's chocolate-macadamia nut cookies.

"I really shouldn't," she said, but accepted one. While they talked, she ate three more.

"Have you had any more luck with Ed's file?" she asked.

He smiled ruefully.

"Why the smile, Jack?" she said. "Don't tell me you figured it out?"

Jack laughed. "I wish. I'm afraid that's one locked file that's going to stay locked."

Cleo frowned. "What do you mean?"

"The disk," Jack said. "It was part of my stuff."

Her eyes widened in surprise. "Part of the stuff that was wrecked?"

"Afraid so."

"What about your computer?"

"What?"

"Your computer. Did they take it?"

"No."

"They didn't wreck it, did they? Please tell me they didn't wreck it."

Jack thought about that for a moment. "I don't think so."

"You don't think so? What do you mean, you don't think so?"

"It looks okay." In fact, it looked fine. But machines were a lot like people. You couldn't always tell just by looking at them whether they were damaged or not. "I haven't turned it on." He hadn't seen any point to it now that the disk was ruined.

"Come on!"

She galloped up the stairs as if she owned the place. When Jack caught up to her, she was already seated at his computer and was reaching around the side to turn it on.

"Thank God," she murmured as letters appeared on the screen. "It's working perfectly."

"For all the good it does me."

She grinned up at him and tapped the keyboard. "Ta-da!"

Jack stared at the file list on the screen, at the file name El, and at the prompt at the bottom of the screen: Password:

"How did you do that?"

"Always back up your file, Jack."

"Huh?"

"Always keep a copy of your file. I copied this one onto your hard disk."

He stared at the screen, then at her, and didn't know what to say. He had resigned himself to never knowing what was on the disk. In fact, he had been a little relieved by its destruction. And now here it was again, like him, miraculously resurrected from the dead.

"Thank you very much, Cleo Taradash," Cleo said sarcastically as he stared speechlessly at the computer terminal. "You're welcome, Jack Thorne." A furrow appeared in her forehead. "Jack Thorne," she murmured.

"That's my name," Jack said.

"What did his mother say Ed talked about all

the time?" She stared at him intently, the look in her eyes one of pure fanaticism. She was starting to remind Jack of some of the guys he'd seen on Four North back in Mercy General. "And what did that snake in the grass Mitch Cameron say he talked about all the time?"

Jack was about to answer "Woodward and Bernstein," when she added:

"Or, should I say, who?"

She was onto something, the gleam in her dark eyes made him sure of that. And suddenly Jack felt clammy all over. What if she actually managed to unlock the disk? What if he found out something about himself that he didn't want to know?

"Look, Cleo . . . "

"It's you, Jack. You're what — I mean, who he talked about all the time." She swivelled around and banged at the keyboard: J A C K.

Beep.

The prompt re-appeared stubbornly on the screen again: Password:

"Damn!" She thumped the desktop with her fist.

"Cleo?"

"I thought I had it, Jack. I thought for a minute I had it. I thought you were the password. The one name he'd never forget." She stared at the screen again. "El," she said. "E-L. Ed Lyle. He named the file after himself. It makes sense that he'd make your name the password."

Jack stared at the file name. She was right. It did make sense. What maybe didn't make sense was being close to something, but being afraid to take the chance to find out what it was.

"My name," he said slowly. "Or my initials."

She grinned and spun to face the screen again.

Tap-tap. J T.

"That's it!" she said triumphantly. "Look, Jack, it's retrieving the file."

Her voice trailed off as the screen filled with letters. Not different letters, not letters broken into words. But the same letter, over and over, filling the screen from left to right, from top to bottom. Xs. A thousand of them.

Cleo hit the page-down key. More Xs. Page-down again. More Xs. She keyed through the file for a few pages, then skipped to the bottom.

"There are three hundred pages in this file, Jack," she said.

"Which makes it about two million Xs." Jack shook his head in disgust. "Well, I guess that's something nobody told us about old Ed. He has a wicked sense of humour."

He felt stupid. Stupid and disappointed. He thought he had come to one of those forks in the road Bugs was always talking about, where he was going to have to make a monumental decision about the course of his life, and really all he was doing was playing some ridiculous game, like a contestant on a TV show. And he was even more ridiculous than the game was. He had chosen door number two — the one that hid the booby prize, the rubber chicken. A disk full of Xs, and none of them marked the spot. He reached over to switch off the computer. Cleo caught his hand and stopped him.

"I want to try something."

"Forget it," Jack said. "It's all some stupid practical joke. There's nothing there. There was never anything there."

"I want to try something," Cleo repeated. She repositioned the cursor at the top of the document and started through the file screen by screen. Page by page.

"You're wasting your time," Jack said. "There's nothing there."

"Ed went to a lot of trouble to lock this file, Jack. There must be something here. It makes sense."

Jack shook his head. "Everything makes sense to you."

She gave him a sour look. And then it appeared on the screen. A grid, it looked like. A diagram of some kind.

"A map," he said out loud.

"Yeah," Cleo said. "But a map of what? Where?"

They scoured each line of each of the three

hundred pages, looking for a clue, a word, something that would tell them what the map meant.

"A very wicked sense of humour," Jack said
softly.

2

"There he is," Jack said.

Mitch was coming down the hallway, an unlit
cigarette hanging out of his mouth, a girl on his
arm.

"Do you have to ask him?" Cleo said, wrin-
kling her nose in distaste.

"If Ed left me a map like that, he must have
expected me to know what it was a map of. Seeing
as I don't, I figure Mitch is the only person left
who might."

"That makes sense," Cleo said grudgingly.

Not for the first time, Jack wondered why she
seemed to dislike Mitch so intensely. She
watched his approach as though it was the slow
but steady onslaught of the plague.

"Well," she said, "if you're determined to talk
to him, I guess now's the time."

"Hey, Jack!" Mitch grinned at Jack. His smile
became jagged when he glanced at Cleo. "Hey,
Jack, have you met Vicki? Vicki, this is Jack.
Vicki's new around here, Jack, and she's very
good in school. Hell, she's very good any place,
you know what I mean, Jack?" He winked.

"Mitch, I need to talk to you."

Mitch glanced at Vicki, then at Cleo. "Sure, Jack," he said. "Why don't you girls run along and fix your makeup or something?" He patted Vicki on the rear.

The gesture worked on Cleo like a red cape in front of a bull. She pulled herself up straight and prepared for battle.

"For your information," she said, "I don't wear makeup."

"Yeah, I can see that, babe," Mitch said. "So why don't you just run along with Vicki? I'm sure she'd be glad to teach you a few tricks."

Cleo's eyes blazed. Jack caught one of her hands in his and squeezed it. Then he turned to Mitch.

"Knock it off. She's my friend."

Mitch stiffened. "I thought I was your friend," he said. "Jeeze, let a guy get a little bump on the head and he all of a sudden can't remember who his best friend is."

Jack took Cleo aside a few steps. "We'll just be a few minutes," he said. "Will you wait for me outside? Really, I won't be long."

She glowered at him as if he had just attempted to run her through with a dagger.

"Please, Cleo?"

"Please, Cleo?" Mitch mimicked in a falsetto. Jack glanced angrily at him.

"Come on, Cleo, five minutes, okay?"

Cleo spun on her heel and, without another word, marched away down the hall.

Mitch patted Vicki on the rear again. "See you later, huh, baby?" He dismissed her easily, then had a hard time tearing his eyes from her swaying hips as she disappeared around a corner.

"So," he said as he turned reluctantly back to Jack. "What can I do for you?"

Jack dug in his pocket for a sheet of computer paper and handed it to Mitch.

"What's this?"

"Look at it," Jack said

Mitch glanced at the paper.

"Yeah, so? What is it?"

"What does it look like?"

Mitch turned the paper around to examine it from a new angle. "Like a bunch of X's on a page." He handed it back to Jack. "What is this, Jack? Some kind of a joke?"

"It's serious," Jack said. "I'm serious. I want you to take a look at it and tell me what you see."

Mitch frowned, but accepted the piece of paper and studied it more carefully. "It looks like some kind of a map."

"That's what I thought," Jack said. Relief washed over him. So he wasn't crazy, they weren't seeing something that wasn't there. Mitch saw it too. "But a map of what?"

Mitch looked surprised. "You mean you don't know?"

Jack shook his head.

"So what do you care what it's a map of?" Mitch said. All of his standard sarcasm disappeared. "Where'd you get this, Jack?"

"From Ed Lyle. I got it from Ed Lyle."

Mitch's face clouded. "Are you feeling okay, Jack? You're not freaking out on me again, are you?"

"I'm fine."

"Then what do you mean you got this from Ed? Ed's ... he's gone, Jack. He took off, remember?"

"It was on that computer disk I told you about."

Mitch looked completely baffled. "But I thought the disk was no good ... I mean, you said you couldn't get into it, that you needed a password but you didn't know what it was. What's going on?" He squinted at Jack. "Did you remember the password, Jack, is that it? Are you getting your memory back?"

Jack shook his head impatiently. "If I'd gotten my memory back, I wouldn't be standing here asking you about this map. Look, Mitch, I have a feeling about this map. It's important. It must be. Ed went to a lot of trouble to hide it."

"And you think maybe it has to do with why Ed took off, is that it?" Mitch rolled his eyes. "Jeeze, Jack, your memory cells weren't the only things that got wiped out in that accident. I think you lost all your smarts cells, too. You should listen to yourself, Jackie. You sound like something out of a spy novel. Coded computer disks, maps where X doesn't just mark the spot, X *is* the spot, any spot you'd care to name. You gotta get a grip on yourself, Jack. This is the real world. In the real world guys don't take off because of something on a coded computer disk. They take off because they've had it up to here with the old lady carping at them all the time."

"Well I guess I don't know the real world," Jack said. "Half the time, I'm not even sure what real is. I don't know what I'm supposed to think, how I'm supposed to feel, how I'm supposed to act around people. People who know me. You probably don't understand, Mitch. I'm not sure what I'd make of a guy like me if I wasn't going through it myself. But I have to find out about this. It's weird, you know, walking around, not really knowing who you are, just walking around. The only thing I remember from . . . before . . . is Ed's face. I have to know about this map. I have to find out why Ed Lyle's face always turns up in my nightmares."

Mitch said nothing for a moment, then finally sighed. He plucked the map from Jack and studied it again. "Jeeze, Jack, the way this is drawn, it could be anywhere on the planet. I don't even see any landmarks."

"There are a few." Jack jabbed a finger at a

spot on the paper. "See this, and this over here?"

Mitch squinted at the map. "Those Xs? Jack, in case you hadn't noticed, this thing is crawling with Xs."

"These are different. These are italic. If you read them as pictures, they give directions. See? North, south. And these here? These are lighter. I think they mark the boundaries of the area mapped. It's a weird kind of shape, though, almost a trapezoid."

"A what?"

"A sort of pushed-over rectangle. Looks like someone kicked its butt."

Mitch looked at it doubtfully. "Yeah, but it still could be just about anywhere."

"If it really is a map, it will lead me to something. Something that Ed wanted to hide so much he buried this map in a locked computer disk. I figure if Ed had something to hide, he'd be sure to hide it in a place he knew pretty well. Not someplace obvious, though, or where it was likely to be found by accident. Mitch, all I'm asking you to do is think about it. You knew Ed and me pretty well, right? Can you think of any place we liked to hang out? All I want to do is find out what this map is all about. Maybe the reason I can't remember is because I don't want to remember."

Mitch frowned. "I thought it was because of the accident. Because of what happened to your head."

"Maybe," Jack said. "They're not a hundred percent sure. Maybe. Maybe not."

Mitch was silent. He shook his head slowly.

"I don't know, Jack. It sure would help if there was a little more to go on."

Jack took the map from Mitch, refolded it, and slipped it back into his pocket. "Will you just think about it? And let me know if you come up with anything. Anything at all, even if it seems far-fetched, okay? I have nothing else to go on."

Mitch shrugged. "Yeah," he said at last. "I guess I could do that. I gotta tell you this though, Jack. You may be my best friend, but I just gotta tell you that I think this whole thing is crazy. I think you ought to relax, I think you should work on your pool game. And I definitely think you should forget about Ed Lyle. The guy didn't even have the decency to drop you a postcard, for pete's sake."

Or maybe, Jack thought, he couldn't drop me a postcard.

"I appreciate your help, Mitch," he said.

Cleo was leaning on the railing just outside the front door of the school. She looked blandly at him. It was impossible for him to tell if she was still angry.

"So, how did it go?"

She didn't sound angry.

"I thought you were mad."

"I was," she said. "At him, not you. He's such

a chauvinist pig. He wouldn't have told you anything with me around."

"He didn't tell me much without you."

"He didn't have any ideas?"

"None."

"I'm sorry." She slipped a hand through his arm. Her touch took the sharp edge off his disappointment.

3

Jack closed the front door behind him and headed for the stairs. He almost jumped out of his skin when the door to John Thorne's study opened and John Thorne himself stepped out.

Half of Jack wanted to bolt up the stairs as fast as he could. The other half wanted to stand his ground, to deny John Thorne the satisfaction of seeing him run. Jack stopped and faced the man who was his father.

John Thorne attempted a smile and failed miserably. He looked like half of him wanted to be some place else, too.

"Hello, Jack," he said.

Jack nodded in acknowledgement.

John Thorne glanced around, like a kid checking the hallway for the school principal. "How would you like to come into my study for a few minutes, Jack? Maybe you and I should talk."

Jack looked John Thorne square in the eye.

John Thorne looked away almost immediately.

"No thanks," Jack said.

The man's face twisted in anguish. "Please, Jack?"

"I don't know what we have to talk about," Jack said. "I don't even know how we can talk. You never look at me. You haven't looked at me since I got here."

John Thorne raised his eyes slowly. They were watery as he looked straight into Jack's own.

"Please, Jack," he said. "It would mean a great deal to me if you'd hear me out. Just this once."

Jack wanted to say no. He didn't know John Thorne very well. Just well enough to realize that he didn't feel the same way about him as he did about his mother.

"Please, Jack?"

It would probably mean a lot to his mother if he at least listened. He followed his stepfather into the panelled study and sat down on a leather armchair. And then he waited. John Thorne was the one who wanted to talk. John Thorne could be the one to start.

John Thorne stood awkwardly in front of his desk, smiling feebly at his son. "It's funny," he said at last. "Here you are, you don't even remember me, and yet you react to me exactly the same way you did the first time you met me." He attempted another smile. This one was even weaker than the first. "I know you don't like me, Jack. Hell, you never liked me. But just because you don't like me, that doesn't mean I'm some kind of murderer. I'm as decent as the next guy. You can ask anyone who knows me. I work hard. I can be a little pig-headed, sure. But I'm a decent guy, Jack. And a decent guy can only stand so much."

He had stopped pacing and was standing right in front of Jack, leaning into him. "She was at that damn hospital every day, Jack. Every day and every night. She wasn't going to go home until she could bring you home, even if it killed her. And then she got sick, and I had to watch her eating away at herself, blaming herself because she couldn't be there every day with you. I couldn't let that go on forever, could I? They said your chances of waking up were slim to none. She would have worried herself to death at your bedside, Jack. I couldn't let that happen. You can understand that, can't you, Jack? Can't you?"

Jack stood up slowly. "I have to go now," he said.

"But you can understand it, can't you? They said you would probably never wake up. I didn't want to lose Elise. You can understand that, can't you, Jack? I didn't want to lose her."

"Sure," Jack said as he edged toward the door. "I can understand that." The lie was bitter on his tongue.

4

Jack's mother stared dreamily into John Thorne's eyes all through supper. She didn't even notice when the telephone rang.

"I'll get it," Thorne said.

Jack jumped up. "No, it's okay. I'll get it." Anything to get away from them for a while.

He picked up the receiver on the fifth ring. "Hello?"

"Jack? Hey, Jack, something came to me."

"Mitch?"

"Yeah. Listen, Jack, I thought about what you said. About the map. Are you still interested, Jack?"

Jack gripped the phone tightly. "Interested in what?"

"What do you think?" Mitch's tone was sharp. "What's the matter, Jack? Having second thoughts?"

"No!" He spoke more loudly than he had intended. His mother looked over at him, her face intent with surprise.

"Jack, who is it?"

"Jack? Hey, Jack, are you there?"

"I'm here," Jack said. But he felt as though he were a hundred kilometres outside his own body. His mouth was as dry as chalk. His heart raced. Mitch had remembered something. What if it was something Jack didn't want to know?

His mother's expression had shifted from surprise to concern. "Who is it, Jack?"

Jack cupped a hand over the mouthpiece. "It's someone from school," he said. "It's about homework."

His mother was visibly relieved.

"Meet me first thing in the morning, Jack. Early as you can. At the gravel pit. You remember where that is?"

"N-no."

He glanced as his mother. She didn't seem to be listening any more. Her attention had reverted to John Thorne. She gazed happily at him over the rim of her wine glass while Jack listened to Mitch describe how to find the gravel pit.

Jack turned his back to his parents. "You don't have to be there," he said into the mouthpiece.

"I know. And you don't have to be there, either. This is stupid, Jack. I mean, think about it? Why would old Ed leave you a map to the old gravel pit? Jeeze, it sounds like some stupid kid's story about pirates and buried treasure."

"Like I said, you don't have to be there."

"Yeah, sure I don't. Because you're the boy genius, right? You know exactly what part of the pits that's a map of, right?"

"Well, uh . . . "

"Early, Jack. I'll be waiting for you."

Before Jack could say another word, the line went dead.

"Is everything okay?" his mother asked when he took his place at the table.

Jack nodded and cut into a piece of Marguerite's lemon chicken even though he was no longer hungry.

"I have a math quiz tomorrow," he said. "That's all."

4

Jack excused himself right after supper and went up to his room. He set his alarm for five, but barely slept. He was up and out before the sun peeked over the horizon, and he loped through the streets, following the directions Mitch had given him to the gravel pit. Just as he arrived at the gate, Mitch climbed out of a black Chevy parked on the side of the road. He opened the trunk and retrieved a shovel.

"You have that map?" he asked.

Jack patted his jacket pocket.

"Well then, I guess we might as well get started," Mitch said. "The sooner we get digging, the sooner we can get this stupid thing over once and for all."

Jack looked at the shovel in Mitch's hand and shuddered. He prayed that it would strike rock, not bone.

"Let me have the map, Jack."

Jack handed the map to Mitch, who studied it for a few minutes.

"Okay." There was a rush of excitement in his voice. "I think we may have something, Jack. Come on."

Jack followed him through the gates and around the wild lip of a vast meandering hole in the earth.

"This way," Mitch said, leading the way through waist-high weeds. "I'm pretty sure Ed's map is of the old pit, the one they abandoned years ago. It figures that Ed would pick a place like that to hide his goodies. Jeeze, I don't think he ever stopped playing cops and robbers."

"Cops and robbers?"

"Well, sheriff and outlaws. The way I heard it, you and Eddie used to hang out here with your toy six-guns and your broom handles — "

"Broom handles?"

"They were supposed to be horses." Mitch grinned. "Get it? You guys used to come out here and play good guys, bad guys. You were always the good guy, of course."

"What were you?"

"I didn't have the pleasure of knowing you in your good-guy days." Mitch laughed. "You two sure must have been a couple of geeks when you were kids. The big difference between you and Ed is, Ed never stopped being a geek."

Mitch climbed up a brush-covered slope and came to a sudden stop. Jack scurried up after him, and almost lost his footing as he crested the slope. The ground suddenly fell away in front of him. He found himself perched precariously at the lip of a yawning chasm in the ground. He teetered slightly at the discovery. Mitch thrust out an arm and grabbed him by the elbow, tugging him back a pace.

"You got to be careful up here," he said. "It's a long way down. And there's no water at the bottom to break your fall."

Jack ventured a look downward — forty or fifty metres downward. His stomach churned. He stepped back another pace.

"There's a trail that leads down this side," Mitch said. "Ed was always referring to this place as Death Valley. You know, like in the Westerns. I bet you anything that stupid map is a map of Death Valley."

The path down was steep and overgrown. Although Mitch loped along easily enough, Jack stumbled more than once. By the time they were halfway to the bottom, he was tired from the exertion.

When they finally reached the floor of the pit, Mitch came to a sudden stop. Jack ploughed into his back. Mitch said nothing. His eyes were sweeping over the nearly barren terrain. He studied the map again.

"Over here, I think," he said, and led the way. "Okay, look, Jack. See that X? And see that big boulder?"

"You mean that outcropping there?"

Mitch nodded.

Jack looked from the map to the chunk of rock Mitch indicated, and nodded.

"Looks like that could be the X that marks the spot, doesn't it?" Mitch said.

Jack reluctantly agreed. "Could be."

"Here," Mitch said, handing him the map. "Hold this, will you?"

Jack shook his head. "I'll dig."

"I'm in better shape."

Jack reached for the shovel. "I'll dig," he said again.

Mitch sighed. "That figures." But he relinquished the shovel to Jack.

5

"Well, it seemed like a good idea," Mitch said. He leaned on the shovel and looked at the three other holes he and Jack had taken turns digging. "It looks as though I was wrong." Unlike Jack, who was perched on top of the landmark boulder, he seemed cheerful. "What do you say we call it a day? If this isn't the place, then I sure don't know what is. And this obviously isn't the place."

Jack jumped down from the boulder and

wiped the dust from the seat of his pants. Maybe Mitch was right. Maybe this wasn't the place. Maybe there wasn't a place. Maybe the whole thing was just some gigantic joke, and Ed Lyle was sitting on a beach somewhere on the coast laughing his head off over the whole stupid thing.

Mitch planted the shovel in a heap of gravel and reached for his jacket. "I don't know about you, Jack, but I sure could use a nice long cold one."

"One more," Jack said.

"Huh?"

"One more hole. I want to dig one more hole." Because what if it really was a map and this really was the place? What if the only reason he didn't find the answer was because he gave up one hole too soon?

"Aw, come on, Jack, we've been digging forever."

"You don't have to stay if you don't want to, but I'm going to dig one more hole." He grabbed the shovel and drove it into the ground a metre or two from the hole that Mitch had just finished.

Mitch clucked in disgust behind him. "You're a stubborn guy, Jack." He hopped up onto the boulder and dug a pack of cigarettes from his pocket. "Some things never change, right?"

Jack rammed the blade of the shovel into the hard ground and pried loose a hunk of earth. He dug single-mindedly, relentlessly, despite the aching muscles in his arms and the burning pull at the base of his spine.

Mitch leaned back and lit a cigarette. "I don't know why you're being so pig-headed about this," he said. "Hell, Jack, I don't even know why you give a damn. The guy was after you all the time, telling you to get to class on time, get to the gym on time, get home to mommy and daddy on time. He wasn't a person, Jack, he was a clock. A grandfather clock — old-fashioned, out of date." He exhaled a cloud of noxious smoke. "Guys like Ed Lyle don't run away to the coast. They run away to places like Ohio. Or Kansas. Places where nothing ever happens."

Jack paused to wipe the sweat from his forehead with the tail of his shirt. "I thought you were friends."

"You were friends, Jackie. You and Ed. I never figured out what you saw in him. The guy had no vision. He wasn't like you and me."

Jack drove the shovel into the ground and jammed a foot on top of it to force it to bite more deeply. "Wasn't?"

Mitch shrugged through a cloud of smoke. "He wasn't when he took off," he said. "Who knows, maybe the guy's changed. I doubt it, though. A leopard doesn't change its spots, right?"

Jack hoisted another shovelful of earth from

the hole. The skin on the inside of his hands burned. He was sure he had raised a couple of dozen blisters. Tomorrow his hands would be so sore he wouldn't be able to close them. He didn't care.

Thunk.

He glanced up at Mitch and saw that he had heard it, too. He had jumped down from the boulder and was crushing out his cigarette.

Jack stooped and groped in the hole with his hands. He had hit something, but what? A rock, probably. His hands clawed through the cold damp earth and felt . . . something smooth, hard and small.

"What is it?" Mitch asked impatiently.

Jack worked around the surfaces of whatever-it-was. A pipe, maybe? No. No, it wasn't a pipe. It was too short for that, and was closed at each end. A can, perhaps. He pried it free from the surrounding earth. It was much, much lighter than he had expected. It was . . . it was a can. A coffee can, sealed at one end with a plastic lid.

"You found it!" Mitch exclaimed.

He had found something, that was for sure. But what? He fumbled with the lid of the can while Mitch looked over his shoulder. "Well?" he demanded impatiently. "What is it? What treasure did old Ed bury?"

Jack pulled out the contents of the can.

"A key?" Mitch stared at it. "Ed hid a key in a coffee can in the middle of Death Valley? What the hell is going on, Jack?"

6

It was a funny kind of key, not like any that Jack could remember seeing before. Instead of being completely flat, like the key to his house or the keys that jangled from a ring on George the orderly's belt on Two East back at Mercy, this key had a rounded plastic head that was stamped with a number.

"Let me see that," Mitch said. He grabbed it from Jack's hand and studied it closely. "Looks like the key to a locker."

"At school, you mean?"

"Not school. The lockers at school all take combination locks, not keys." Mitch turned the key over and over in his hand. "Looks more like a key to a locker in a bus station. What do you suppose old Ed might have put in a locker at a bus station?"

"Whatever it is, it must be pretty important," Jack said.

"Important? What would Ed be doing with something important?" Mitch shook his head. "I keep telling you, Jack, the guy was a complete loser. He had these big dreams of being some hotshot reporter, but, jeeze, he couldn't even get himself a regular beat on the school newspaper. He wrote up the sports scores, that was all they trusted him with. How could a guy like that have anything to do with something important?"

"Why would he go to so much trouble to hide this key if it wasn't something important?"

"You're like a bulldog, you know that, Jack? Now that you've latched onto this one, you're not going to let it go, are you?" Mitch sighed. "Okay, you win. Come on, I'll drive you there."

Jack frowned. "Drive me where?"

"To the bus station. To put this thing to rest once and for all. But if you don't mind, I have to make a pit stop. It's been a long morning, you know?"

They stopped at Hy's Gas and Grub. Mitch dug in his pocket and pulled out a couple of loose bills which he pressed into Jack's hand.

"Gas it up, will you, Jack, while I go take a leak. Hey, you hungry? I'm hungry. I'll get us something to eat, okay?"

Before Jack could answer, Mitch loped around the side of the gas station.

Jack passed the money on to the gas bar attendant who turned out to be Hy himself. Then, as he waited for Mitch, he looked at the key again, and wondered what secret it might unlock. Or whether, as Mitch had predicted, it would only prove him a fool. After all, Mitch knew more about Ed Lyle than Jack did — a lot more. Jack wasn't even sure he would be able to pick Ed out of a lineup at this point. So it made sense that if Mitch thought they were on a fool's errand, they probably were. But Jack couldn't shake the idea that he had to follow the trail to the end. He had to find out for sure.

When Mitch finally emerged from the restaurant attached to Hy's garage, he was carrying a brown paper bag and wearing a grim expression.

"What's the matter?" Jack asked.

"What?"

"You look so serious all of a sudden."

"Guess I need a caffeine fix." He handed the paper bag through the open window to Jack, and swung around to the driver's side. Jack fished out a cardboard container of coffee and handed it to Mitch, who peeled back the lid and gulped some down.

"Hand me a dog, will you?"

Jack pulled out one of two hot dogs wrapped in heavy paper.

"Chili dogs?" he said in surprise as Mitch ripped off the paper.

"Best in town." Mitch grinned and took a bite.

Jack bit into his own and had to admit it tasted pretty good. So good that it was gone in no time.

Mitch crumpled the wrapping paper and crammed it into his empty coffee container. He leaned back in the driver's seat and burped with contentment. "Just what the doctor ordered," he said as he turned the key in the ignition.

Ten minutes later, Mitch pulled up in front of a parking meter across the street from the bus station. He fed a quarter into the meter, pulled on the crank, then turned to Jack and said, "Ready?"

Ready as I'll ever be, Jack thought. He nodded and they started across the street, side by side.

7

"I don't get it," Mitch said in exasperation. "This has to be the place. Look, it's the same kind of key. So where the hell is BP608?"

They had walked the length and breadth of the bus station twice, and checked every single one of the more than a thousand lockers that lined the walls. There was no BP608. Jack glanced over at the main counter where a lone clerk sat, watching them between ticket sales.

"Maybe we should ask," Jack suggested.

"No!"

"Why not? Maybe there are some more lockers in here that we don't know about. If we ask — "

"No."

"I'm going to ask." Jack strode to the counter

before Mitch could say another word. "Excuse me?"

The grey-haired man behind the counter peered through thick glasses at first Jack, and then Mitch, who had scrambled after him.

"Excuse me," Jack said again, "but could you please tell us where I'd find locker BP608?"

The man's bland expression soured. "Well it ain't here, that's for sure," he said.

"But it has to be here. I have the key." He held the key out. The man barely glanced at it.

"That ain't a key from here."

"What do you mean it ain't a key from here?" Mitch said. "Of course it's a key from here. It looks exactly like every other key in this whole friggin' place."

The man's lips curled upward in a bitter smile. "Maybe you need glasses, son," he said, "because that key ain't like the others at all. That's a BP key. Bus station keys don't have BP on them. Bus station keys only have one letter on them. N series keys are for the lockers on the north side of the station, S for lockers on the south side of the station, W — "

"I get the picture," Mitch said irritably.

" — for lockers on the west side of the station," the man continued, "and E for lockers on the east side of the station. There are no BP series keys in this bus terminal."

Mitch's fist hammered onto the counter.

"Damn!"

Yeah, Jack thought. And double damn. He looked at the man behind the counter, who seemed smug now, rather than sour.

"Do you know where we might find lockers with BP series keys?" he asked.

"I might," the man said with annoying calm.

Jack felt Mitch coming to a slow boil beside him, and lay a restraining arm on his wrist to stop him from doing or saying anything to antagonize the man. "I'd appreciate it," he went on, "if you could tell me where I could find the locker this key fits. A friend of mine, a real practical joker, borrowed some stuff of mine, left it in a locker, and mailed me the key."

He couldn't tell whether the man behind the counter believed him or even cared if he was telling the truth.

"Try Bernie's Place," the man said.

"Bernie's place?"

"I know where it is," Mitch said. "Come on, let's go."

He was off and running for the car before Jack even had a chance to thank the man.

"Who's Bernie?" Jack asked as he slid into the passenger seat. He hadn't even shut the door before Mitch pumped down on the accelerator and they went squealing out of the bus station parking lot.

"It's a place," Mitch said. "Bernie's Place is

this place, they cash cheques there for people who don't have bank accounts. They rent out boxes for people like the post office, you know, for people who don't want to get their mail at home or don't have a home to get mail at. And they rent out lockers."

<h1 style="text-align:center">8</h1>

From the outside, Bernie's Place looked like a 7-Eleven. It was brightly lit and the plate glass windows that enclosed it were papered with splashy signs in neon colours. But instead of hyping the cost of nachos and cheese or the weekly special on cigarettes, these signs advertised *Cheques Cashed, No Account Necessary*, and *Storage By The Week, By The Month, By The Year.*

Jack followed Mitch inside, and glanced around. A couple of guys were over by the mail boxes. One was just opening his box, the other was ripping open an envelope. There was only one customer at the *Cheques Cashed Here* counter, a woman in a dismal housedress and a baggy cardigan sweater. She was laboriously endorsing the back of a cheque while a bald-headed man behind the counter puffed on a cigarette. Jack hurried after Mitch as Mitch headed for the area marked *Storage*.

Lockers of various sizes lined the walls of the storage area from floor to ceiling. Two rows of lockers back to back completed the floor plan.

Mitch ran to the closest locker that still had a key in it. "This is it!" he said. "BP608. This is the place!" He hurried down the wall of lockers, his finger running over the number plates. Jack scrambled along behind him.

"Five-eighty-eight . . . six-oh-two . . . six-oh-EIGHT! This is it, Jack! We found it! Give me the key."

Jack dug in his pocket for the key, but did not hand it over.

"If you don't mind," he said, "I'd like to open it myself." In fact, he wanted to open it alone, to face alone whatever it might contain. If, he reminded himself grimly, it contained anything at all.

Mitch shrugged and nodded. "Okay. Sure," he said. He laughed. "I'm getting to be as crazy as you. I really got caught up in this thing, didn't I?"

The key burned in Jack's hand. As he inserted it in the lock, he noticed his hand was trembling. He stared for a moment at the small square door. It looked like every other dull yellow locker door on the wall, nothing to be afraid of. But doors weren't the problem. The problem was what they hid. Jack drew in a deep breath and turned the key in the lock. Or rather, tried to turn it. The key wouldn't give.

"What's the matter?" Mitch asked. "Why don't you open it?"

Jack tried again. The key still didn't turn. It didn't even seem to fit all the way into the lock. "I don't think this is the right locker. Or else it's not the right key."

"How can it not be the right key?" Mitch asked. He looked exasperated. "It says BP608. This is locker BP608. Of course it's the right lock and the right locker. Maybe you just have to jiggle it a little. Here, give me that."

Mitch grabbed the key from Jack's hand and rammed it into the lock. It wouldn't turn for him either, although he twisted it so hard Jack was afraid it was going to snap. Then Mitch pounded on the locker.

"Hey, hey, HEY!" shouted someone behind them. A man came out from behind the cash counter. He was carrying a baseball bat. "Hey, knock that the hell off," he shouted, "before I knock your head the hell off."

"Are you Bernie?" Jack asked.

The man looked startled. "No. I'm Fred. Bernie's dead."

"I'm sorry," Jack said.

"Then you obviously didn't know him," Fred said. "And you don't know me, either, if you think you can kick in my lockers and not get your head kicked in. You want to get into a locker, you need a key. You don't have a key, you get the hell out of here."

"We have a key," Jack said. He took the key

from Mitch and held it out to Fred. "It just doesn't seem to work."

Fred squinted at the key. "Here, let me see that."

"Don't give it to him," Mitch said.

Jack handed him the key. Fred studied it a moment. "That's one of mine, all right. Here." He handed the baseball bat to Jack and tried the key in the lock. "You're right. It doesn't fit. When did you boys rent this locker, anyway?"

Jack opened his mouth to say he wasn't sure, but Mitch beat him to it. "About a year ago."

The man snorted and returned the key to Jack in exchange for the baseball bat.

"A year ago. I bet your rent ran out. When someone's rent runs out and they don't renew and they don't return the key, I have to change the lock."

"What about the stuff that was in there?" Jack said. "What did you do with that?"

"Probably sold whatever was good and threw the rest out," Mitch said bitterly.

"Hey," the man said, waving his bat at Mitch, "just because the people who use my services don't have stockbrokers and chauffeured limousines, doesn't mean I'm some kind of a crook. You want the stuff you left in there, it's probably in the back room. I just bag it and throw it all in the back room till it's claimed. Or till I have no more space left, whichever comes first.

You want to look through it and find your stuff, it's okay by me. Only you have to sign for it, so I know where it went, in case it turns out you decide to help yourself to someone else's stuff while you're in there. Okay?"

"Okay."

The back room was hardly more than a closet. It was lined on three sides with shelves, each of which was crammed with bags and boxes and parcels. There was barely room for Mitch and Jack to squeeze inside.

Jack stared at all of the parcels and wondered who had abandoned them, and why. Then he turned to Fred. "What kind of order is this stuff in?" he asked.

"Order?" Fred laughed. "It's in the order of wherever I could find a space to cram it, that's what order it's in."

"Well, is it at least numbered? Maybe with the locker number?"

Fred shook his head.

Mitch groaned. "Great," he said after Fred had left them alone with the job. "This could take all day."

"You've been a big help," Jack said. "I never would have got this far without you. But you don't have to stay now. I can take it from here. It's okay."

"Not stay?" Mitch looked appalled at the suggestion. "How can I not stay?" He stared up at the uppermost shelves. "Just let me go out and have a quick smoke, then we'll dive right into this, okay?"

"Okay," Jack said.

Mitch wasn't gone long. "Did you find anything yet?" he said as he squeezed into the room. Jack shook his head.

"We don't even know what we're looking for, do we?" Mitch said.

Jack shook his head again.

"Well," Mitch went on, "I guess there's only one way to do the job, and that's to do the job. What have you done so far?"

Jack nodded toward the topmost shelf.

"Okay," Mitch said. He knelt down and started at the bottom.

They worked in silence for five minutes, and then five minutes more, opening the plastic bags into which Fred had emptied the smaller lockers, prying open the boxes which held the larger items. It was funny, Jack thought, what kind of things people had put into storage and had never returned for. Bundles of clothing, pairs of boots, books, records, musical instruments — a flute, a saxophone, a pair of maracas.

"Jeeze," said Mitch, "look at this!" He held up a filmy red brassiere while Jack undid the tie on yet another plastic bag. It contained only one item, a bulky envelope. "And this!" Mitch said.

"There's a suitcase full of this stuff, you wouldn't believe it."

Jack pulled the envelope from the bag and read the writing on the outside.

"Either some hooker stashed her booty here," Mitch continued, "or some pervert."

Jack's knees buckled.

"Hey, Jack," Mitch said, "hey, are you listening to me? You haven't even looked at this stuff. It's unbelievable stuff, Jackie!"

"I-I think I found it." Something deep inside him had pushed him to this point. He knew Ed Lyle, knew him from before. When everything else about his life had deserted him, Ed Lyle had held fast. Ed Lyle had been with him every night, in his dreams. Maybe he'd even been there in the dark times, the times when Jack had existed but when he hadn't lived. It was possible, just possible, that Ed could help him recall himself. It was also possible, Jack knew only too well, that he might recall something that was best left forgotten.

Mitch jumped up. "Found what? What is it?"

Jack's hand trembled as he held out the envelope for Mitch to read. *To be opened on my death.*

Mitch laughed. "You're getting spooked again, Jack. What makes you think that's even from Ed? Probably some weirdo left it here. Probably a cousin of the guy who left all the lingerie."

Grimly, Jack turned the envelope over. Imprinted neatly in black ink on the back flap were a name and address — Ed Lyle's name and address.

"What did I tell you?" Mitch said, rolling his eyes in disgust. "Jeeze, if that isn't just like Ed. He always had to blow everything up, make a big deal out of stuff that never was a big deal. To be opened on my death! Maybe the guy was barking up the wrong tree trying to write serious journalism, maybe he should have tried writing for the funny pages!"

Jack blinked in surprise. "You mean you don't think this is serious?"

"Serious? *To be opened on my death?* Come on, Jackie, don't tell me you think it's serious? You were out too long, pal." He took the envelope from Jack. "What do you say we file this in the old circular file and get out of here? I don't know about you, but I could use a serious meal right about now."

"Give me back the envelope, Mitch."

"Come on, Jack, enough is enough. We dug up his stupid little treasure. We played his stupid little game. Now let's get out of here and get a bite to eat, okay?"

"You can go if you want," Jack said. "Just give me back the envelope."

Mitch kicked a carton on the floor of the storeroom.

"Jeeze, Ed's a pain in the butt. He's not even here and he's a pain in the butt." He sighed and handed the envelope to Jack. "So, go ahead," he said. "You might as well open it."

Jack slipped a thumb under one corner of the flap and tore the envelope open.

"Well?" Mitch said, "What is it?"

"A notebook," Jack said. He flipped through page after page filled with cramped handwriting. "And another envelope."

"A notebook? What kind of notebook? What's in it?"

"I don't know. The big one."

"What do you mean, the big one?"

Jack held out one of the pages. Across it someone, Ed, had scrawled *This is the BIG One!* Big was triple underlined.

"Terrific," Mitch said. "The big what? The big wild-goose chase?"

Jack thumbed more slowly through the pages. He was getting accustomed to Ed's tight hand, and was starting to follow the thread that ran through the notes.

"Maybe the big story," he said, glancing at Mitch.

Mitch almost choked on his laughter. "The big story? Jeeze, Jack, Ed's gone, but that doesn't mean you have to take his place."

"I'm serious," Jack said. "He's got dates here, and places. A parking lot down by the lake, the parking lot of something called Chicken King . . ."

"The best fried chicken in town," Mitch said.

" . . . the alley behind . . . " His voice trailed off. He flipped back a few pages, then forward again.

"The alley behind what? Hey, earth to Jack, are you reading me, Jackie?"

"What's Gary's last name?"

"What?"

"Gary. That guy you hang out with down at the pool hall. What's his last name?"

"Parker. But what's Gary have to do with this?"

"One of the people he's writing about is a G.P. Gary Parker."

"Or George Potter. Or Gus Pus. Or Gopher Piss."

"This G.P. was in the alley behind Mario's pool hall."

"Well in that case, maybe G.P. stands for Garbage Pail. Come on, Jack, let's get out of here. Let's go get something to eat."

Jack didn't move. "If these notes are for real, maybe Ed didn't just run away. Maybe he was scared away. Maybe worse."

"What are you talking about?" Mitch said impatiently. "For pete's sake, Jack, you're starting to sound just like Ed."

"Then why don't you take a look?" Jack

handed the notebook to Mitch, who started to flip through it. The pages turned more slowly the more he read. "Maybe they found out that Ed was on to them," Jack said. "Maybe Gary and — "

"G.P.," Mitch said. "You don't know that Gary has anything to do with this. Hell, you don't even know if there really is a G.P. For all you know, these notes are some stupid story Ed was making up."

"Maybe," Jack said. But that wouldn't explain his dreams, and so he didn't want to believe it. "Or maybe this G.P. and this other guy, this L.M., found out that Ed knew. Who do you know with the initials L.M.? Those guys who hang around with Gary, what are their names?"

"Pete and Len."

"Len! That could be it."

"Len Arnoy," Mitch said. "L.A., not L.M."

"Come on," Jack said. "I don't know whether this is real or not. Maybe you're right. But maybe you're not, Mitch. Don't you want to find out for sure?"

"What I want to do for sure," Mitch said, "is get something to eat and forget I ever knew Ed Lyle. Jeeze, look what he's done to you — got you running all around like some hotshot TV private eye. Well, this isn't TV, Jack, and you're no P.I., and Gary isn't some major criminal, so what do you say we take this notebook and dump it in the closest G.P. and get ourselves out of here?"

A tremor ran through Jack, and for a moment he was illuminated. I know, he thought. I know. But the moment flickered and was gone, and he realized that he knew nothing at all. He stared a moment at the notebook in Mitch's hand, then took it from Mitch and tucked it and the second, smaller envelope back into the larger envelope in which he had found them.

"I want to know more," he said. He backed out of the tiny storeroom and headed to the nearest exit from Bernie's Place, waving his thanks to Fred at the counter as he went.

"Hey!" Fred called. "Hey, did you find your stuff? If you found your stuff, you have to sign for it."

Jack shook his head. He didn't want to stop to sign anything. He wanted to find out what was going on. And there was only one way he knew of to do that.

"Hey!" Mitch called as he ran to catch up with him. "Hey, wait up!"

Jack shouldered his way out a side door and into the parking lot.

"Hey!" Mitch caught him by the arm. "Don't be stupid, Jack. Gary's not the kind of guy you want to mess with, not even on a good day. If you go near Gary with a story like that you'll stir him up so bad it won't matter whether he did what Ed says or not, he'll still kick your face in."

"I'm not taking it to Gary," Jack said. "I'm taking it to the police."

"What?"

"I'm taking it to the police."

"They'll laugh you out of the cop shop."

"I don't care."

Mitch's face lost its good humour. "You're acting like a real jackass, you know that? We ought to just dump that stuff and forget the whole thing." He made a grab for the envelope Jack was carrying. Jack pulled it smartly back out of his reach.

"I'm going to the police, Mitch. You don't have to go with me."

"You don't have to go with me," Ed said.

"I said I'd go with you, didn't I?" Jack asked, exasperated. "I'll go with you."

"No."

"Ed —"

"No, Jack. I have to go alone."

"You don't have to go with me," Jack said, "but you're not going to stop me."

Mitch made another grab for the envelope, and missed. As Jack turned, he saw a familiar face coming toward him. Here was someone who could help.

"Hello, Jack," Lieutenant Mahoney said. Then, in a less friendly tone, "Hello, Cameron."

Mitch stared icily at the lieutenant.

"There's something I wanted to talk to you about," Jack said.

Mahoney smiled pleasantly. "Well, here I am."

Jack glanced around dubiously. "Here?"

"Would you rather go to my office? I have my car here."

"I have my car, too," Mitch said quickly. "How about we meet you there?"

"Why waste gas?" Mahoney said affably. "Come on, Jack, I'll drive."

"No!" Mitch grabbed at Jack. "We'll take my car, Jack."

The amiable smile slipped from Mahoney's face. "I don't think so, Cameron," he said.

Mitch sneered in defiance. He opened his mouth to say something, then quickly closed it again. His cockiness vanished. He stared mutely at the service revolver that Mahoney had pointed directly at him.

"H-hey," Jack started to say.

"Walk slowly across the parking lot, boys, and everything will be just fine. Make any trouble and, well," he shrugged, "I'd just hate to have to shoot someone who was resisting arrest."

"Arrest?" Jack said.

"Walk," Mahoney said.

Jack glanced at Mitch, who scowled back at him. They started slowly across the parking lot.

"What do you mean, you have to go alone?"

"There's some stuff going on in the department, Jack. It's all very hush-hush. I shouldn't even be telling you. But there's some stuff going on in the Department and he says Internal Affairs is involved."

Jack's mouth gaped as he stared at his friend. He liked Ed, he really did. They had been friends since kindergarten. But did he always have to act like such a goof?

"Who says?" Jack said. "And what are you talking about, Internal Affairs? What's Internal Affairs?"

"They're the cops who investigate the cops. If there's a cop who's on the take, or a cop who does something illegal — "

"You're telling me that you're going off to meet some cop in the middle of the night all alone because there's something kinky going on in the Police Department? Come on, Ed. Get real. This all sounds like something out of a movie. And a pretty bad movie at that."

Ed fixed him with a serious look. "This is no movie, Jack. This is for real. And there is something going on. Something really serious."

"L.M.," Jack said. "Lieutenant Mahoney."

Mitch stopped walking to stare at him.

"Come on," Mahoney growled. "Keep moving." He shoved Mitch. Mitch stumbled forward.

Jack thought about the gun Mahoney was holding. Would he really use it? If Jack made a run for it, would Mahoney really shoot him?

A woman got out of a car a short distance away and started into Bernie's Place. What if I shout? Jack thought. If I shouted and got that lady's attention, what could Mahoney do? He wouldn't shoot us in front of witnesses, would he? Jack glanced at Mahoney, whose face was deadly serious. Would he?

The woman pulled open the door to Bernie's Place and disappeared inside.

"Okay, stop," Mahoney said.

They stopped in front of a black four-door. Jack stooped to get a look at the driver. His heart clenched as he peered through the window. It was Gary.

"Open the door, Cameron," Mahoney said. Then, "You, Jack, you get in first."

Jack glanced at Mitch, who looked grimly back, then opened the back door and started to climb in.

"Wait a minute," Mahoney said. "Hand them over."

Jack tried a puzzled look. "Them?"

"Don't give me that," Mahoney said. "You know what I'm talking about. The pictures."

Mitch sounded surprised. "There were pictures?"

Mahoney paid him no attention. His eyes

were on Jack. They burned into him. "Come on, Jack, don't be a fool. Hand them over. Before I hurt your friend here."

"Hey, wait a minute," Mitch said.

Mahoney's eyes didn't waver from Jack's. "It's up to you, Jack. Hand them over now, or I'll hurt your friend and then I'll hurt you and I'll get those pictures anyway."

Jack handed him the envelope.

"Now get in," Mahoney said, waving at the car with his gun.

Jack climbed into the back of the car. Mitch climbed in beside him. Then Mahoney got into the front seat and swivelled around to train the gun on them. He nodded curtly at Gary. "Let's get out of here."

Mahoney held the gun on them while Gary drove east, out of town. Mahoney dug into his jacket pocket and pulled out a pair of handcuffs. He tossed them to Mitch, who stared at them as if they were a coiled snake.

"Cuff him," Mahoney said.

Mitch just looked at him.

"I said, cuff him."

Mitch reached for Jack's wrist.

"Behind his back," Mahoney said.

Mitch pulled Jack's arm behind his back. Jack jerked free.

"Don't do it," he said. "If he wants to tie us up, let him do it himself."

Mahoney pointed his gun at Jack's head. "Be a good boy, Jack, and put your hands behind your back."

Mitch twitched nervously as Mahoney cocked the gun. "Do it, Jack," he said. "He means business."

"But . . ."

The fear in Mitch's eyes worked like acid on Jack's resolve. He went momentarily limp, and a chill ran through him as he allowed Mitch to pull his arms behind his back and handcuff him.

Mahoney nodded with satisfaction, uncocked his revolver, slid it back into its holster, and opened the envelope he had taken from Jack.

A flash of panic surged through Jack's body. Now that he was restrained, Mahoney had relaxed. Even though Mitch was still free. Realization washed cruelly over Jack. He stared bitterly at his friend.

"Are they there?" Gary asked, glancing from the road to Mahoney. "Did you get the negatives this time?"

"Yeah," Mahoney said. "I got them." He flipped through the small stack of photographs that the second envelope contained. "This time when I burn these babies, they're going to stay burned."

"Yeah, well, this time we had some professionals on the case. Right, Mitch?" Gary said. "This time we're going to take care of business, just like we took care of Lyle."

Jack looked only at Mitch. "You're going to let them do this, aren't you?" he said. "You're not even going to try to stop it."

"Stop it?" Mahoney laughed. "That's a good one. Why would Cameron want to stop it? If anyone's got a reason to make it happen, he does." He tossed the stack of photos into Jack's lap. Several of them skidded to the floor. A couple of them landed on the leg of his jeans. In one of them, between Mahoney and another guy, was Mitch.

This time when Jack looked at Mitch, Mitch met his look.

"I can't help it, Jack," he said. "I'm in raw sewage up to my chin. If I don't stand on somebody, I'm going to drown."

Jack went numb all over. His voice echoed in his ears from a million light-years away. "You said you were my friend," he said.

"I am your friend," Mitch responded. "But what can I do, Jack? It's you or me, Jack. You or me."

If you're not going to tell me where you're going and you're not going to tell me who you're going to meet and you don't want me to go with you, why are you even here, Ed? Why aren't you out there playing undercover cop or investigative reporter or whatever it is you play?"

"I told you, Jack. This is big. And I have to be careful. I'm only taking copies of the evidence with me. I hid the originals."

Jack shook his head. "You sound strange, Ed. You sound like a psycho."

"I'm not asking you to do much, Jack. You don't have to do anything at all if you don't want to. But I'd appreciate it if you would hang onto this for me. Just in case."

He handed a computer disk to Jack.

9

They left the hardtop and crunched over a gravel road that Jack did not recall ever having travelled. Mitch refused to look him in the eye now. He sat sullenly beside Jack, staring out the window.

After a while, the gravel turned to heavily rutted dirt. Gary slowed the car and navigated the ruts and potholes like a ship's captain navigating a treacherous reef. *Whump!* The car's undercarriage slammed onto the hard ground. The car rocked.

"Take it easy, will you?" Mahoney snarled. "You're going to kill the suspension."

"Take it easy yourself," Gary said. "You're going to blow a gasket."

Jack glanced at the back of Gary's head, then at the lock button, which was depressed. Slowly

Jack eased his shackled arms to his left, as close to the door handle as he could bring them without twisting his body and calling attention to himself. He looked up at Gary and Lieutenant Mahoney. Both were hunched forward in their seats, watching the road. Mitch still refused to look at Jack. Just as well, Jack thought.

In one fluid movement, he wrenched his arms sideways and turned the handle, while at the same time ducking and clamping his teeth around the button. Just then, the car slammed into another pothole and Jack's teeth smashed into the metalwork of the door frame. He felt something snap inside his mouth, and tasted the salty sweetness of his own blood.

"Watch it, you idiot," Mahoney roared.

Jack had broken a tooth and sliced open his lip, but he didn't let his injuries stop him. This was his chance. Maybe his only chance. Mitch started to turn his head. Jack clamped his good teeth around the lock button and yanked it up. The car door swung open and Jack tumbled to the hard-packed dirt road.

Gary slammed on the brakes before Jack could even scramble to his feet. Jack had barely staggered off the road when he heard three car doors open, then, like a volley of cannon, bang shut again. He forced himself to concentrate on the underbrush that stretched away from the road. To look back would be to waste precious moments. His only chance lay in lengthening the distance between himself and Mahoney.

He heard their footsteps and their breathing behind him.

"Bring him down," Mahoney was shouting. "I don't care how you do it, but bring him down."

The ragged earth swept upward. Jack's lungs burned as he forced his legs to pump harder and harder, to carry him up the steep slope, to keep him out in front.

Something reached up, caught his leg, and held it. Jack felt himself toppling forward. With his arms still fastened behind him, there was nothing to break his fall. He hit the ground all at once, his legs, his belly, his torso, and — because he twisted to keep from falling on his face — his shoulder. His entire right side seared with pain as his body made contact. He heard something crack, and thought he had broken his shoulder. Maybe Mahoney heard it, too. Maybe that was why he got Gary to grab Jack by the handcuffs and jerk him brutally to his feet. Jack felt as though his arm had been ripped from its socket.

Mahoney stood in front of him, his face twisted with rage. "It's too bad that truck came by when it did, Jack," he said. "If it hadn't, no one would have seen your wrecked car. No one would have seen me there when it exploded into flame."

The image that shimmered in front of Jack's eyes rattled him. "They told me you saved me," he said out of his confusion.

"Saved you?" Gary laughed. "That's a good one." He shoved Jack. "You're going in the right direction. Keep walking."

Jack stumbled onward, higher and higher, until suddenly the trees ended and the earth fell away. He looked down into a deep ravine and remembered . . .

. . . looking up through the trees. They were easy to see through, then. It was well into autumn and the leaves had fallen. He could see two figures up at the edge of the ravine. One was Ed, who stood facing him. Jack could only see the back of the other figure. The cop. The guy Ed was meeting. Jack crouched behind a tree to watch. What could go wrong when a guy was meeting a cop? But why here? Why were they meeting way out here in the middle of nowhere?

Ed seemed to be talking. He took something out of his pocket and handed it to the cop. Then, slowly, he turned toward the ravine. Jack frowned. What was he doing? Jeeze, it looked like he was going to jump, but that couldn't be right. He couldn't be going to jump. Then something flashed, the reflection caught Jack in the eyes, and for a moment he was blinded. His vision cleared just in time to see Ed disappearing into the ravine.

It couldn't be happening. Jack started to run

toward the edge of the ravine. Then the cop turned. Sweet Jesus, the cop had a gun. That's what had made Ed jump. Jack turned and thundered down the slope.

He heard the cop calling behind him, and then came the sound of footsteps crunching over dead leaves. He forced his legs to pump harder. His car was just down below. If he could just make it to his car . . .

"Stop him," the cop yelled. "He's going for his car, stop him!"

Who was he shouting at? How many of them were there, anyway? Jack glanced wildly around and saw another figure running up the hill toward him. More cops? Then he recognized one of them. That guy Gary Parker who hung out down at Mario's. Someone else was coming up the hill. Thank God, he thought, opening his mouth to shout. Thank God Mitch was here. Mitch would help him.

"You killed him," Jack said. He stood at the lip of the ravine, as Ed had done, and faced Mahoney and his gun. "You killed Ed. Why?"

"The kid knew too much," Mahoney said.

"What a joke, huh?" Gary said. "The guy was a complete idiot, a real airhead, and he had to die because he knew too much. Who would have thought, huh?"

Jack glanced at Mitch, who was standing off

to one side and refusing to meet his eyes.

"He wouldn't have known anything if you hadn't been shooting off your big mouth down at Mario's," Mahoney said to Gary.

"Then what's in that notebook is right. You really are involved in drug smuggling. Cocaine, he said. A cop heading a cocaine smuggling ring."

"What difference does it make, Jack?" Mahoney said. "Knowledge is like everything else in this world. You can't take it with you. Turn around, Jack."

Jack didn't move. "What did you do with his body?"

"Same thing we're going to do with yours, Jack," Gary said. "We buried it."

"Turn around, Jack."

Jack didn't move, couldn't have moved even if he wanted to. He felt like he was in a dream, one of the ones where no matter how fast you run and where you try to hide, the horror always finds you, until you start falling and falling . . .

"Okay," Mahoney said, shrugging with resignation. "You don't want to do this the easy way, I guess we'll just have to do it the hard way."

He raised his revolver and cocked it.

I could make a break for it, Jack thought. He wouldn't get far, there was no possibility of that. But he could at least try. He could at least refuse to let it end without even a fight.

"Last chance, Jack," Mahoney said.

Every muscle in Jack's body tensed. Now, he thought, and dove forward, his legs propelling him headfirst towards Gary. Might as well try to do some damage, he thought. Might as well try to do some hurting of his own.

A gunshot exploded in his ear. Then another. Jack hit the ground hard, missing Gary, who seemed to be moving in slow motion now. Everything seemed to be moving in slow motion. Mitch and Mahoney were rolling on the ground. With every revolution, Mahoney's gun glinted in the sunlight. Gary headed toward them, oblivious now to Jack. Jack staggered to his feet and started after him. As Gary grabbed Mitch and started to pull him off Mahoney, Jack bent for another attack. This time he took careful aim, and caught Gary full in the kidney with his head. Gary fell like a rock. Mahoney and Mitch continued to grapple on the ground until the gun rang out again, twice.

EIGHT

*To know after absence the familiar
street and road and village and house
is to know again the satisfaction of
home.*

Hal Borland
"Homecoming - August 29"
Sundial of the Seasons

1

A tube ran from a needle embedded in Mitch's arm up to a plastic bag filled with clear liquid suspended from a pole at the head of his bed. Mitch's face was as white as the pillow his head rested on, but he managed a smile when Jack came into the room. Jack didn't smile back.

"Good to see you, Jack." His voice was hoarse and raspy. "Hell, I'm even glad to see her." He nodded at Cleo, who was standing at Jack's side. "Jeeze, am I ever thirsty."

Jack glanced at the uniformed police officer sitting on a chair just inside the door.

"Can I give him some water?"

The policeman nodded, and watched carefully as Jack poured water into a cup and held the straw to Mitch's dry lips. Mitch drank greedily.

"I really am glad to see you, Jack," he said. "For a while there, I thought I was finished. I thought that was it — goodnight Mitchell Cameron."

Jack put the cup back down onto the bedside table.

"How are you feeling, Mitch?"

Mitch attempted a shrug and winced in pain as a result. "Okay, I guess. Better than I felt when I thought I was going to die."

Jack glanced at the policeman on the chair, then back at Mitch. "What's going to happen now?"

The smile faded from Mitch's lips. "My lawyer was here this morning. My dad said he's a good defense attorney, one of the best. But he didn't sound very optimistic, Jack." He closed his eyes for a moment, and looked suddenly small. When he opened them again, none of their familiar old sparkle was evident. "I can't believe this is happening to me, Jack. It's like the night Ed died. I couldn't believe that was happening, either. I was just there, you know. I was there and it happened right in front of me, before I could do anything about it. Jeeze, I could end up in prison. I could — " His voice choked off and he sniffed, then looked away. It took him a few moments, but he found a shaky smile and put it on. "How about you, Jack? How's it going with you? Are you back to your old self yet?"

"You mean, do I remember?"

Mitch nodded.

"No," Jack said. He struggled to keep the disappointment out of his voice. When the excitement had died down, after the police had come, after Mahoney and Gary had been packed into the rear of a police cruiser, after Mitch had been loaded into the ambulance, Jack's heart was racing. He had remembered. He had seen visions, true pictures from the past, and he had greeted the images as if they were trailers in a movie theatre, teasers, *Coming soon to a memory near you.* But the past hadn't come flooding back to him. Except for a few split-second highlights, what he had been still eluded him.

"You don't remember anything?" Mitch asked.

"Hardly anything. And what I do remember, I wish I didn't."

"I hope the stuff you remember about me is the good stuff," Mitch said. He tried to laugh, but ended up coughing instead. Pain flickered in his eyes. He smiled up at Jack through clenched teeth.

The police officer in the corner got to his feet. "Your time's up," he said to Jack. "You'll have to go."

Jack nodded. "I just wanted to see if you were

okay," he said, "And to thank you for what you did this time."

"Yeah, sure," Mitch said. "What are friends for, right?" His lips were white as he attempted another smile. "Hey, who knows, maybe the judge will go easy on me because of it."

"Maybe," Jack said. "Maybe if you had done the same thing for Ed, things would have turned out differently. See you around, Mitch."

"Yeah," Mitch said.

2

"Now what?" Cleo asked as they left the hospital.

"Now," Jack said, "I'd like to go home. And I'd like you to come with me. I think it's time you met my parents."

"Your parents?" Cleo looked a little nervous. "What if they don't like me?"

"If my father doesn't like you, you have to watch out," Jack said. "But my mother will love you. She's always wanted me to find a nice girl."

"Always?" Cleo's eyes narrowed suspiciously.

"For as long as I can remember."